KING PIANKHI 2

Tut's Revenge

Written and Edited

by

Michael K. Jones

PARENTAL ADVISORY EXPLICIT CONTENT

Warning:
Read *King Piankhi* first.

King Piankhi,
The First Black Pharaoh
It explains some parts of this book.

Copyright © 2020 by Michael K. Jones

All rights reserved.

This is a work of fiction. All events and characters in this story are solely the product of the author's imagination. Any similarities between any characters and situations presented in this book to any individuals, living or dead, or actual places and situations are purely coincidental.

Without limiting the rights under copyright reserved above, no part of this manuscript may be reproduced, stored in or introduced into a retrieval system, or transmitted in any form or by any means (electronic, mechanical, photocopying, recording or other-wise), without the prior written permission of the copyright owner.

ISBN-13: 9798616608314

www.kylesarmy.com

Chapters

1. The Departure
2. I'm Dinner
3. Atlantis
4. The Kidnapping
5. The Trip
6. The Long Flight
7. Operation High Jump
8. Surrender
9. The Tong
10. The Bet
11. Revenge and Rescue
12. The Ride to A-Town
13. Run

2 Edras 6:9

Prologue
(True)

Starting in 1928 Richard E. Byrd, a Naval ***Medal of Honor*** recipient, explored the Antarctic on many dangerous expeditions. He became most famous for flying over the North Pole in 1926. What people don't know is, in 1946 he commanded a three naval battle group known as ***Operation High Jump*** down to the South Pole and got his ass kicked.

The official fabricated report is he lost only one plane and three Navy men. Many believed they were hunting Nazi's, but this **homophobic** book explains what really happened.

Egypt 2010

(End of King Piankhi Part 1)

Five hours after the Giza Pyramid was bombed, the sun rose quickly as the desert heat amplified the rise of mirage inducing thermal waves.

Two unmarked F-35 fighters were in full afterburner at low altitude trailing an Egyptian armored personnel carrier that hovered above the sand and traveled at a higher rate of speed.

The jet on the right fired an in-bay sidewinder missile that supersonically flew and exploded to the right of the vehicle. Then the truck began to increase its speed as the second F-35 fired an Aim-120 missile from its underbelly bay.

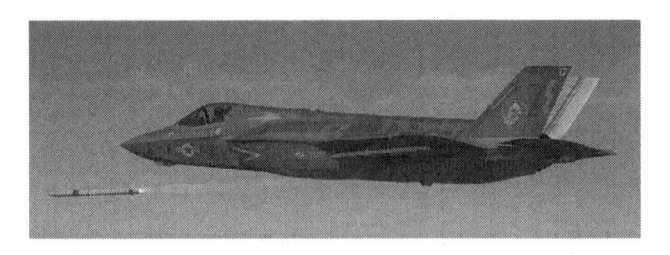

The missile was dead on target as the troop carrier then accelerated twice its speed causing the electronic tracking to disengage. The missile then crashed and exploded into a nearby sand dune. It was believed that the carrier was piloted by the injured King Tut as the two fighter jets under orders, suddenly bugged out and flew back in the opposite direction.

The next day the Egyptian Government explained that the pyramid light show witnessed the night before by thousands was a test for the upcoming *Eid al-Fitr* (End of Ramadan Fasting) celebration which will include more fireworks. Nobody believed that as rumors began to circulate that Israeli jets were seen flying at a low altitude toward the pyramid and bombed a tour bus full of Syrians.

King Piankhi's mummy was given to the Museum of Sudan and placed in isolation until it was tested and authenticated that it was the lost ruler of Nubia.

Anand and Nafy went into hiding in Khartoum knowing King Tutankhamen would seek revenge for the breaking of Canuk's legs and destroying their only means of contacting their home planet. They had a small wedding at the Ali Saeed Mosque in north Khartoum performed by Hassan Al-Turabe, a local political leader.

Hassan Al-Turabe
Born 1932 / Died 2016

Famous Sudanese scholar and lawyer

After the ceremonies, they both stayed at a secure location on the outskirts of the city. Paid scouts, some grateful volunteers, kept a vigil eye out for anything suspicious at different locations all across Khartoum. Kintu had a plan for his brother that would regain his freedom, and not be cooked and hog-tied on a table with hungry cannibals eating his eye-balls and testicles smothered in a savory bowl of beef broth.

Chapter 1

The Departure
2011

A year had passed as Anand and Nafy began to feel the frustrations of indoor confinement. Registered under false names, the two had moved from hotel to hotel under the cover of darkness. It was a cool fall night at 10:35 pm when the arguments began again.

"I can't live like this anymore!" yelled Nafy as she pulled off her head scarf and began combing her nappy hair. "I want to go home…in the daylight."

"Nafy be patient," solemnly responded Anand. "As soon as my brother gets the passports, we are flying far away to live a normal life."

"It better be soon or you'll be sleeping alone," she threatened while walking into the bathroom. "I'm not on their menu."

"I think we both are," said Anand.

"Oh no…you broke Canuk's legs. I just took the amulet."

"It doesn't matter," said Anand as a knock on the door turned their heads in fear.

"It's me…Kintu."

"Thank God," said Nafy as she exited the bathroom bra-less while putting on Anand's t-shirt. He opened the door as an armed guard looked over Kintu's shoulder, smiling toward Nafy's hard nipples.

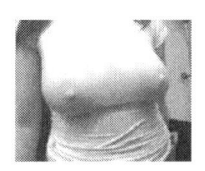

"Pack your things," Kintu said nervously. "A fast moving truck was spotted north of the city."

"Was it Egyptian?" asked Nafy.

"Yes and heading this way."

"Oh shit," said Anand as a thought of his barbequed body on an Egyptian dinner table entered his mind.

"I have your passports and booked a flight to America," said Kintu.

"Where?" asked Nafy while putting on a dress and head scarf in the bathroom.

"Atlanta."

"I wanted to go to New York," she whined disappointingly. Kintu opened another suitcase and began throwing clothes in it.

"We will go someday my love," said Anand, holding her red period panties up that smelled like tuna fish.

"They all were escorted by the guard to a parked van and jumped in quickly. It had a twelve passenger capacity as they ruggedly sped away from the hotel. Kintu followed in his car as the two vehicles headed for the airport. Anand seemed a little worried as Nafy was just glad to get out of the hotel, smiling a few times as the city lights reminded her of the pagan American Christmas holiday.

"I think I'm going to love America," she said while looking at her scared husband.

"Yeah...me too," lied Anand remembering the racist white people in every state he visited. He only felt comfortable in Atlanta confirming that whites there abided in southern hospitality to all races.

He dared not venture into the southern cities of Georgia that flew *Confederate* flags, hearing stories that people of color including white Jews were not welcomed. "I have been to Atlanta and you will love it Nafy. The people are friendly there."

"I always heard that New York is exciting," she said while daydreaming.

"It's too expensive to live there," said Anand as the van swerved while quickly turning down a street. They were three kilometers (1.8 miles) from Khartoum International Airport when a pickup truck began to speed up from behind. The van driver's phone began ringing and he answered it...then quickly hung up.

"Your brother said he is being followed," said the driver while glancing back in his rear view mirror. Anand looked back as Kintu's headlights began flashing. It was the signal to cut off the van's headlights and take the alternate route. Kintu slammed on the brakes as the pursuer's crashed into his trunk that deployed their airbags. He then lost control and crashed into a light pole as Anand's mouth opened in shock.

"We have to go back!" yelled Anand. "My brother crashed!"

"I've been told to not stop for anything," said the driver. "You are important to all Sudanese for returning our king."

"Stop the van!" yelled Nafy.

"No," shouted the driver. "We have a fully armed backup vehicle two kilometers behind us. They will take care of your brother." Anand worried for his brother. Five minutes later, the driver's cell phone rang again. He then glanced at Anand. "Your brother is okay...and they have the two men from the pickup truck."

"Were they Egyptian?" asked Anand.

"Yes."

"They really want to eat you," said Nafy as the driver opened the van door and pulled out their luggage. "Sudanese meat must really taste good."

"Very funny."

"Go to concourse C and sit at the bar," said the driver. "Our men are there and will protect you until you board."

Anand and Nafy hurried into the airport and made it through customs an hour and a half later. They sat at the *Only for Foreigners Bar* as their flight was to board twenty minutes later. Anand wanted a drink so badly but had to adhere to the **Islamic Sharia law** that prohibited any locals from consuming alcohol. He just stared at a departing tourist turn up an overpriced imported beer and remembered the taste from his college days. He then couldn't wait to get back to America, to shove one down his throat.

Khartoum Airport

They later boarded the flight to Atlanta without incident and Anand was relieved. It was until an announcement the pilot made during the flight that scared him. The plane was experiencing flight control problems in the rear stabilizer and they had to emergency land in Benghazi, Libya.

"I don't like this Nafy," Anand said a little nervous. "I bet you King Tut is alive and waiting for us at the Libyan terminal…with a knife and fork."

"You are assuming too much."

"Maybe you're right," said Anand as the plane was leaving Egyptian airspace. He then remembered the Alexandria stabbing in his arm and he believed in the distance, he saw the actual city lights along the coastline.

He knew Alexandria was directly across the border, east from Benghazi along the Mediterranean coast line. The plane landed and all the passengers were ordered off as several Libyan mechanics that looked like Egyptians swarmed the plane on the tarmac.

As Anand and Nafy walked through the concourse doors from the tarmac, they were grabbed by local uniformed officers affiliated with Interpol (International Police).

"Why are you arresting us?" asked Nafy as they handcuffed both of them.

"I knew it," said Anand. The officers didn't say a word as they were pushed and seated onto a terminal golf cart. They quickly rode thru the terminal and were ordered into a room at customs. Their hands were handcuffed to chairs and ten minutes later, an officer entered and ordered them to be quiet as he sat down and began writing. He obviously didn't like Nafy because she was a woman.

"I know my rights," she said angrily. "You can't arrest us for no apparent reason."

"Nafy...please be quiet," said Anand.

"This is not Egypt and you *are* not under arrest," said the officer. "But your husband is. He stole a priceless artifact from Germany."

"What are you talking about?" lied Anand. "I…I didn't steal anything."

"It says here…you broke a museum tablet."

"Not me."

"I'm looking at a photo of you kicking its case over."

"It was an accident."

"Did you accidently kiss that tour guide?"

"What!" yelled Nafy. "You said the tour guide was a man."

"Don't listen to him Nafy…it was for the mission."

"Was it your mission to kiss that Ethiopian woman in Shendi?"

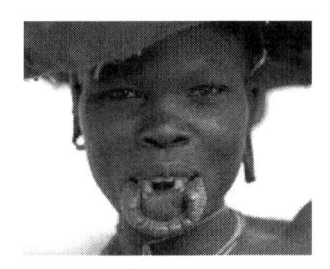

"That was horrible, I mean she kissed me."

"Kintu was right. I can't trust you."

"I assure you…those girls meant nothing to me."

"Where's the ankh…Mr. Anand?"

"I thought you said I broke a tablet?"

"We are only looking for the priceless Egyptian artifact."

"You must be working for that fat man?"

The door to the room swung open as an obese man with a lit cigar in his mouth entered.

"I know that smell," said Anand. "It's a Cuban *Limitado* cigar…and you're still fat."

"Mr. Abbul, I see you have a nose for exquisite cigars."

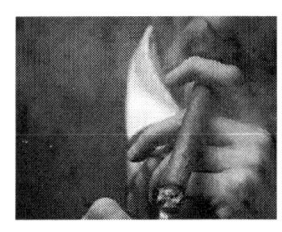

"And I remembered your whole body smelling like camel shit…or was it zebra?"

"Enough with the insults…that fake ankh cost me a lot of money and now we are going to get it back."

"I don't have any money."

"That's why you're flying back to Egypt."

"Why?" asked Anand.

"You have a hefty ransom on your head and the only way you can get me to not collect it…is by giving me the real golden ankh."

"King Tut has it," shouted Nafy.

"Then…we are going for a long ride," said the fat man as the same *big fingered* Ethiopian and another henchman entered the room. "Take them to the *King*."

Nafy and Anand were inconspicuously driven to a hanger and thrown into a large metal cargo container, still handcuffed and then blind folded.

"That black *King Tut* is still alive," said Anand. "And I'm going to be on his dinner table real soon."

"Stop thinking negative," said Nafy. "Just worry about the moment." *Glad I wasn't driving that truck.* "We have to try and escape before they **shish kabob** you through your ass and out your mouth."

"And that wasn't negative?"

"Oh sorry…it just popped into my head."

Chapter 2

I'm Dinner

Anand and Nafy were sure they were going to freeze to death in the cargo container when the plane reached a high altitude. They felt the container being loaded and then heard the sound of a hydraulic door closing.

"I think we are on a C-130 cargo transport," said Anand. "If I'm correct…it will take us 2 maybe 3 hours to get to Cairo."

"How do you know we are going to Cairo?"

"All cargo is flown to *Borg El Arad* cargo terminal…and if the military is involved, we may land at Almaza Air Base which is nearby."

"I hope you're right," Nafy said nervously. "We may be able to escape and make it back to Sudan."

The plane took off 10 minutes later and flew for three hours before landing roughly.

Anand knew it was not on a paved runway but on compressed sand.

They were at a newly under-construction Egyptian military airbase, but where he asked himself.

The two, still blindfolded were pulled from the container and escorted to a one story building near the runway. Anand could smell food he didn't recognize.

"I hope that isn't a barbequed human," said Nafy as she was being pulled by the arm.
"I'm next," said Anand.
"Quiet!" yelled a voice from behind them.
"That must be the cook," whispered Nafy.

They entered a small windowless room as two henchmen began removing the handcuffs and blindfolds.

"I know you two," said Anand while squinting.

The Ethiopian then back-hand smacked Anand like a prostitute. Nafy became angry.

The Ethiopian then reached to his partner that was carrying a black trash bag. "Put these on," he said angrily. "We're going for a long ride."

"I'm not wearing men's diapers," said Nafy. The Ethiopian then pulled out a Taser.

"Put them on…or I will for you."

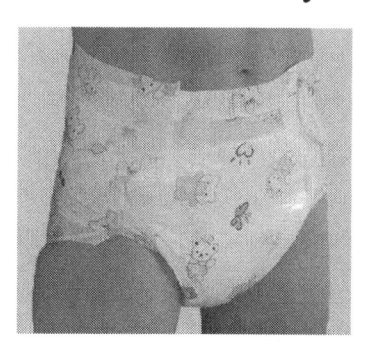

Anand reached into trash the bag and handed Nafy one. You have five minutes before we return."

"The last time I went on a ride with this dude, I pissed my pants on purpose."

"I'm not going to ask why."

"They were assholes and were going to kill me."

"They might kill us both anyway. We have to escape the first chance we get."

"I have a plan," said Anand. "I'm going…"

The door swung open. "Shut up and get those diapers on."

"Fuck you," whispered Anand as he pulled the tight fitting diaper up his legs.

Three minutes later, they were dressed and the Ethiopian and his partner escorted them to a black 2002 M-Class Mercedes.

They pushed them into the back seat and child-locked the doors. "If you try and piss in *this* car Mr. Abbul, I will throw you out of the window at 140 kilometers an hour." (80 mph)

"Then…you better stop at a rest stop because this diaper is going to fill up quick."

Ten minutes later, they drove onto a highway Anand didn't recognize. "Where are we going?" he asked.

"You don't have to worry about that," said the partner.

"We're going to a shit hole," said the Ethiopian. Both men began to laugh.

"That wasn't funny," said Nafy.

"I think they're laughing at me when they pulled an ankh out my ass."

"Out of what?"

"I hid a gold ankh ☥ up my butt to get through customs when I left Germany. They pulled it out…real hard."

Two hours later while driving through an endless desert. The Ethiopian pulled over and Nafy became frightened as the partner removed his pistol from his jacket. He then pointed it at Anand as the Ethiopian took a piss on the side of the road. He returned and his partner then took him one.

"I have to go too," said Anand. The Ethiopian then started the car.

"You can go anytime you want," he said as he drove back onto the desert highway.

"Motherfucker," whispered Anand.

"I peed twice already," said Nafy.

They drove two more hours and Anand saw his first highway sign. It said *Al Hawat Road* and they were heading westbound. He believed they were driving back to Libya because it was the only highway that headed toward the border. Four hours later they began seeing resort signs everywhere as they got closer to Egypt's largest lake on the west coast. The car then veered off the highway and ten minutes later parked behind the Cleopatra Hotel in the Siwa Oasis area.

The Ethiopian and his partner both got out of the car. "Wait here and watch them," said the Ethiopian. The partner stood there for two minutes then the Ethiopian exited the hotel. "Bring the female in first."

"What are you doing Anand?"

"It's called payback honey." Anand pulled down his pants and diaper. He leaned forward, arched his back, and shitted in the seat as the partner opened Nafy's locked door.

"What is that smell?" shouted the partner as he saw Anand leaning over the front seat with his ass exposed.

"Do you have any tissue?" sarcastically asked Anand as Nafy held her nose closed.

"You are the most nastiest man I've ever known," said the partner as he pulled Nafy out of the car. "Raku is going to be pissed."

"Great idea," said Anand. He then pissed on the opposite seat. The partner pulled Nafy by the arm to the other side of the car and opened the door. He pulled his gun out and pointed it at Anand. "Get out of the car…and if you try anything, I'm going to shoot you and then your wife." Anand got out and pulled his pants up. "Start walking," said the partner holding the gun to Nafy's ribcage.

"I said bring the female first!" yelled the Ethiopian as he exited the hotel door again.

"He just took a shit in your car."

"What…oh no he didn't."

"Yes I did," said Anand with a smile. A worried look fell across the Ethiopian's face as he began to run toward his car. He then looked at the backseat and shrugged in anger.

"I'm going to kill him," said the Ethiopian as the partner entered the hotel. He then told the hotel guards already there, to take Anand to her. They did as the Ethiopian entered the doorway with his gun drawn. He was breathing heavily as his anger grew in intensity.

"I know you're mad, but we were ordered to bring him alive."

"I should shoot his wife."

"You don't want to end up on the Prince's table smothered in a garlic butter sauce."

"If Tut doesn't kill him…I will."

"I think he's already on his menu."

Anand was escorted one level down a flight of stairs and then had to walk through a series of guarded locked doors. He finally entered a large open room with one chair and began to remember what happened to him during the ankh extraction incident. *I'm going to get stabbed or eaten alive.* He thought in fear while thinking about his wife. Once again the men kicked the back of his legs, forcing him to kneel. A door swung open and it was Nefertiti, the ugly one.

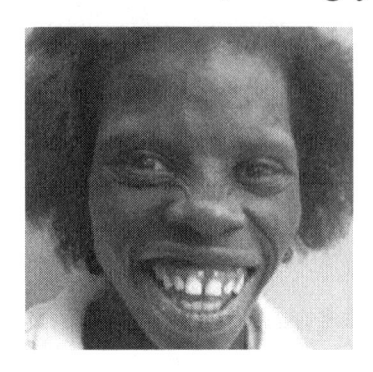

She walked slowly to the chair and sat gracefully, like a queen should.

"Mr. Abbul, first I would like to say thank you for finding the *Ankh* and releasing us from our long sleep in the sarcophagus's." Anand smiled at her unplanned lisp but remained silent. He then became scared wondering if she also had a taste for human flesh.

"You were helped by my son in finding your King Piankhi and later turned against him with help from the American military."

"Your son lied to me."

"Silence!" yelled Nefertiti. Then a guard smacked the back of Anand's neck.

"My son was badly injured, but managed to send the energy from the amplifier we needed. Thousands of years had passed and because of you, we can complete our mission." Anand's fear subsided a little until she spoke about Canuk. "Tutankhamen's actions were out of line and his punishment has already been decided. But what disturbs us now is…why or rather when did our people start eating humans for retribution?" Anand looked confused as to whether he should answer her. "You may speak," she ordered.

"I don't know the answer to your question, but I have read that humans taste like pork and our eyes like cherry tomatoes."

"You have been summoned to Atlantis because you drove the car that shattered Canuk's legs and he is seeking retribution. He is demanding that you be put in an oven, baked for four hours at 350 degrees, and then served to him on a plate with smothered onions." Anand swallowed hard as fear entered his soul again.

"I steered away from him because he was holding my wife," said Anand. "She broke loose and his legs were already weak from chasing her."

"You will have your say in front of my husband. It is he who will decide whether you are to be eaten or not."

"Are you talking about Akhenaten?"

"Yes," said Nefertiti as she stood up to leave. "No one is to harm our guest until he reaches Atlanta." Anand was confused as his head was pushed to look towards the floor as she exited the room.

I'm going to Atlanta? He thought as a fart slipped out of his ass. *We were heading that way in the first place.*

Anand was then picked up and pushed to walk. He reached the entry hall and ran to Nafy as the Ethiopian had just returned from his car. He had rubber gloves on and his sleeves were rolled up. "Were you washing your car?" asked Anand while smiling. The Ethiopian rushed toward him while grabbing his gun from his back.

The three guards that escorted Anand jumped in front of him.

"He is not to be touched," shouted one guard as they pushed the Ethiopian back. He turned away in anger, holding his gun that pointed toward the floor as Anand hugged Nafy.

"What did they say?" she asked.

"It was only Tutankhamen and his servant Canuk that were eating people. I just talked to his mom."

"She is alive too?"

"And his father," said Anand. "He will decide if Tut and Canuk can eat me."

"Where is his father?"

"In Atlanta."

"Isn't that where we were going?"

"I think she meant Atlantis."

About ten minutes later, the Ethiopian finished cleaning the shit and piss out of his new used car and was ordered *under protest,* to drive them to Siwa Lake to the Tahaghien Island Hotel. Nafy and Anand were treated to an Egyptian cuisine and later escorted to a hut shaped tourist suite that had two queen size beds.

"This maybe our only chance to escape," whispered Nafy as she looked out the room window at the guard.

"When the sun goes down, I will create a diversion and want you to run for help." whispered Anand. "Get far away, then find a cell phone and call my brother."

"I'm not leaving you."

"I have to go with them," said Anand.

"Why?"

"I want to see Akhenaten."

"They may all be cannibals," Nafy said with concern. "And you are a buffet."

"If what I read about Akhenaten is true...he will not let them eat me."

"What did you read?" Nafy asked angrily.

"I remember only one of his quotes. *Indulge not thyself in the passion of anger; it is whetting a sword to wound thine own beast, or murder thy friend.*"

"That just means," said Nafy. "Don't be mad and kill your own animals or friends."

"It means he is wise and filled with wisdom enough to be persuaded."

"I'm going to see him too."

"If we are both dead, no one will know what happened to us." Nafy began to sulk. "I need you to tell my brother where we are. He will know what to do."

Chapter 3

Atlantis

Nafy decided to take a shower as Anand sat on the room bed, to think about a good diversion. He planned to fake a stomach ache and run from the hut. He then laid on his back and wondered how he would look on a dinner table.

"Delicious," he whispered "Like a plate of Koshari."

I found this picture on Facebook.

The sound of the shower was soothing as he closed his eyes and unknowingly fell asleep.

Ten minutes later Anand woke up still hearing the shower.

"Honey...are you okay?" he yelled. There was no response. Anand then sat up in the bed again. "Nafy!" he yelled while getting a little concerned. He walked into the bathroom as steam made it hard to see her behind the shower curtain. As he got closer, he realized she was gone. Nafy had burst a hole in the wall and escaped. Anand returned to the room, sat on the bed, and hoped she would managed to get off the island. *I wonder how far Atlantis is from here?* He thought. Then he heard a noise in the bathroom. "Nafy," he shouted with concern. She was on the floor and sweating.

"I made the call and told him where we were."

"How?"

"I found a young man with a cell phone and told him my dad was worried and I needed to tell him we arrived okay."

"Why didn't you escape off the island?"

"I saw your Ethiopian friend's car parked in front of the resort. I think he was still in the lobby."

Meanwhile at that very same time in Khartoum, two suspicious individuals were breaking into and robbing the National Museum of Sudan. It was closed for the day as the men broke in from the back and ran straight to King Piankhi's sarcophagus. They pried it open then pushed the cover to the side while one of the robbers stood over the wrapped mummy.

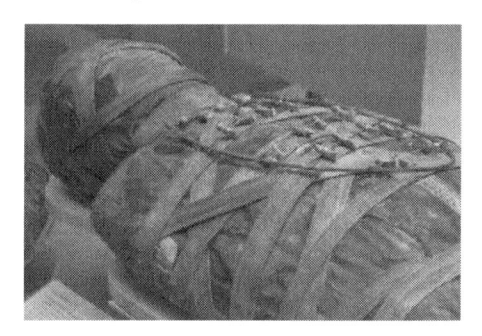

He then reached behind and into King Piankhi's waistline and pulled out a long object. It was heavy but smooth with small carvings on its side.

"Was that up the king's ass?" asked the other robber in Arabic.

"I don't care, but it does have a shitty brown stain around the edges," said the leader. He then put it back and retrieved the item he was told to find. "Those Egyptians really want this thing."

"Let's get the cover back on and get the fuck out of here," said the partner.

The two men ran and the leader stopped at a sword that caught his eye.

"This Kaskara (sword) is mine," he whispered to himself while breaking the glass case. He then placed the sword's strap around his shoulder to carry. His partner was already at the back door, too scared to grab anything. He knew that if they were caught he would be ankle chained like an American Civil War slave and unwillingly sucking dick in about a week.

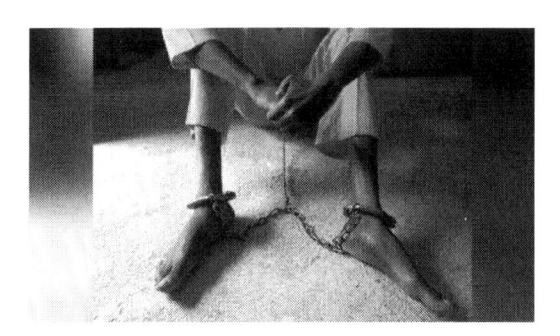

Three days later, the men followed their previous plans and were to meet their Egyptian client at the *Mask Bar and Bistro* in Juba, Sudan. Obviously they wore a mask as they entered the bar with smiles on their faces, knowing they were about to get paid. Both men walked to the bar and order a drink in celebration.

"I am buying my girlfriend a *Loo* roll."

"A what?" asked the leader. "Is that a Sambusa?" (Triangle shape eggroll)

"No, it is roll of soft toilet paper. Her ass is delicate and she has never used any."

"I'm buying…wait a minute," said the leader. "What has she been wiping her ass with?" Then his prepaid cell phone began vibrating and he read a recently sent text.

"The meeting location has been change."

"Where?"

"Drink up, we got to meet him at the bridge." The two men downed their drinks quickly and left the bar.

They drove to a secluded area near the *Blue Nile Bridge* and met a different Egyptian man. He was tall and ugly; holding a briefcase they knew carried their money.

"Do you have the artifact?"

"Yes we do," said the smiling leader, pulling it out of a plastic bag.

"You men were told to retrieve one item from the mummy."

"We did," said the leader. "It's long with etchings, like you said."

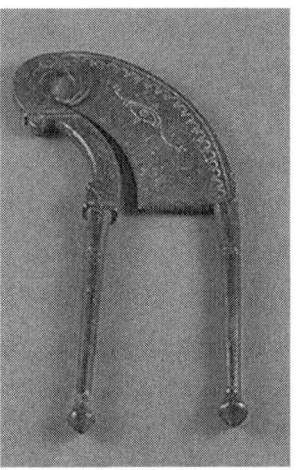

Betel Nut Cutter

"That *Betel* is not the right item," said the Egyptian.

"I think they wanted the dildo," said the partner.

"You also took a Kaskara."

"What's a *Betel*?" asked the leader.

Betel Seeds

When chewed produces a caffeine or nicotine affect.

"You were only ordered to retrieve the **Tong** and now the S.S. police are getting involved." (Sudanese Secret Police)

"This isn't the Tong?" asked the leader.

"Your payment is **null-and-void**," said the Egyptian as he reached into his briefcase.

"What does that mean?" asked the partner.

"Our initial agreement is invalid," said the Egyptian as he pointed what looked like a toy gun. He then fired a red beam at the two men and their faces began to melt off.

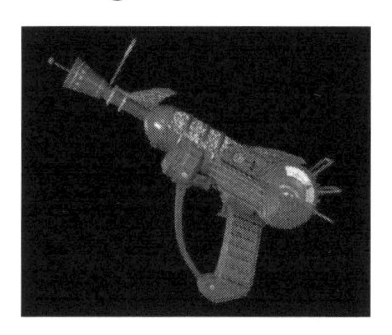

They both screamed in horror as they fell to the ground and shook like detoxing crack whores. Seconds later they died painfully from shock.

****

Back at Siwa Lake, at the Tahaghien Island Hotel, Nafy and Anand were ordered to leave their room because of the hole in the wall. It was 3:35 a.m. when they were escorted to the middle of the island, to what looked like an open fresh water reservoir that was pumped in from the main land. It was quiet and dark as all the tourist seemed to be asleep.

They stood in front of four guards, close to edge of the embankment and Anand feared they were both going to be pushed in.

"I can't swim," whispered Nafy.

"I will help you," said Anand as the water began to bubble. He then for a second thought he was going to be boiled alive until his skin fell off.

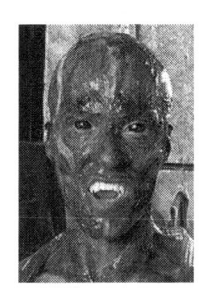

Twenty seconds later a glass tube with a door rose from the water and a ramp extended. They only pushed Anand to walk on the ramp and into the glass tube as two guards followed. "Let my wife come!"

"No," said one guard. The door closed and the other guard stepped on a floor button. The tube began to submerge as Anand solemnly watch Nafy begin to cry. The tube descended slowly as hydrogen and helium was pumped in. Anand became a little dizzy and almost passed out.

Midgets in the Wizard of Oz.

"I think I'm going to be sick," he said sounding like a Munchkin from the Wizard of Oz. The helium reduced the amount of nitrogen in his body to minimize the chances of narcosis developing in him.

> Narcosis is when deep-sea divers become drowsy, go into a drunken state of mind, or even unconscious.

The tube then descended into a underwater canyon and Anand's mouth opened wide with amazement.

"This has to be a dream," he whispered. "Is this the Lost city of Atlantis."

"No, now shut the fuck up." Anand knew that some believed the city was lost somewhere in northwest Africa.

Chapter 4

Kidnapping

The glass elevator stopped in front of a long hallway. Anand was pushed again to walk as he looked through an interior window to his right. He saw a room filled with art work from ancient countries that didn't exist anymore. He then looked ahead of the guards to his left and saw rows of shelves filled with paper scrolls. Then he remembered reading about the great *Library of Alexandria* in northern Egypt that burned to the ground. It was filled with the works from Homer, Plato, Socrates, and many other great scholars. *I bet you that bastard Tut torched that library...after he robbed it.* Anand knew it was Julius Ceasar who ordered the fires to be set (True).

They reached another elevator and Anand hoped it wasn't heading to the kitchen. They entered and the elevator door closed and then opened. They were on another floor at the blink of an eye. He was pushed out and ordered to walk toward a golden door with what he thought were pillars of alien skulls.

The door slid open to the right and Anand's mouth opened wide again. King Akhenaten was sitting on a throne five feet (1.5 meters) high above the main floor.

He must be seven-foot tall. Thought Anand while being pushed again to the floor to kneel. King Akhenaten just stared at Anand as he knew to only keep his eyes looking down. The king then remained silent as the golden door slowly closed, screeching as the sound echoed throughout the whole chamber. The guards rose from their kneeling position as the king stared across the room like a blind man.

"Rise subservient," said King Akhenaten in modern day Arabic. Anand slowly stood not making eye contact.

Your momma's subservient. He thought as the king coughed like a chain smoking Edomite. (White People)

"We are grateful for your lineage's assistance in reviving my family," said King Akhenaten in his native ancient *Demotic* language.

"I don't understand what you're saying."

"Silence," shouted one of the guards as he smacked Anand across the back of his neck. The King then continued in Arabic.

"My son has requested you for consumption with his servant. I have denied him this because he has abused his power." The king coughed again and Anand knew something was wrong. "Because of my admonishment of my son, he has taken control of Atlantis." A tall man then entered the chamber looking like Canuk's brother. He whispered into the King's ear and he paused in confusion, like President George Bush did at that school when the planes flew into the World Trade Center towers.

"We need your help again," said the King. "We must have the artifact in three days…and it is hidden in your king."

"King Piankhi?" Anand asked loudly. He was then smacked again on the back of his neck. *Does my neck have a target on it?*

"You will only speak when the king ask," said the guard.

"You must retrieve the **Tong** and return it here. When you do, we will release your mate unharmed and protect you from my son. You may speak."

"What does the Tong look like your eminence?" asked Anand while thinking about a Chinese gang called the *Tongs*.

"You are to address me as Pharaoh, but I know this world has gotten arrogant. You will not be skinned alive and drained on ice."

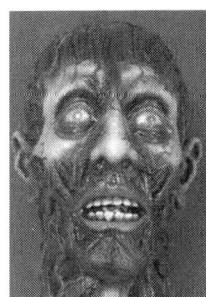

Red algae grows in Antarctic ice.

"Thank you King Pharaoh, but you never answered my question."

"Pharaoh Akhenaten…dumb-ass. Give him the code and returned him to the surface."

The guards then kneeled as Anand followed. They escorted him out of the chamber and he was glad he was not going to be eaten. *I know Akhenaten's dying.* Thought Anand. *And he didn't tell me what the Tong looked like.*

They reached the surface and Anand was locked in a different hotel hut with two guards outside of his door.

The next morning he was driven back to Alexandria and then flown to Khartoum on a commercial flight. He did not shit or piss in the car since they had sheets of plastic covering the entire back seat.

Anand was worried about his wife and ran to the first pay phone at the airport when the guards let him go. He dialed Nafy's cell-phone number first and there was no answer. He then called his brother.

"Kintu...Kintu," he shouted as he looked in both directions on the concourse.

"Little brother are you and Nafy alright?"

"No...didn't she call you?"

"No she didn't. Are you in Atlanta?"

"No...they still have her."

"Who has her?"

"King Tut's dad."

"What are you talking about?"

"They hi-jacked our plane and flew us to a new base in the Egyptian desert."

"Say no more...where are you now?"

"Khartoum airport, Concourse D."

"Go to *Arrivals* at the Sudan Airways baggage claim. Wait for a red Honda Civic."

"Why?"

"Just do it."

An hour later, Anand was picked up by Akmed, his brother's best friend.

"Get in Anand and duck down."

"Akmed...I haven't seen you since I graduated *Unity* high school."

"Hurry, your brother said you are in danger."

"I'm on a mission."

"Just keep your head down until we are clear of the airport."

They reached the safe house and Kintu was in bed with two broken ribs. He was shirtless and completely bandaged around his torso.

"Hey big brother...how are you feeling?"

"I'm okay, now tell me what happened?"

"We were driven to a resort called Tahaghien Island somewhere in the Egyptian desert. There, I was taken to the sunken city of Atlantis."

"One of King Tut's men paid us a visit at dad's old house," said Kintu.

"Akhenaten said his son Tut was upset for not letting him eat me."

"I believe he still wants to," said Kintu.

"What mission are you on," asked Akmed

"King Akhenaten wants me to find this artifact from King Piankhi's sarcophagus."

"What item?" asked Kintu.

"I don't know," said Anand. "It's called a Tong."

"Akmed, find out where this Tahaghien Resort is and send two scouts to surveillance the area."

"I have to pick up the men from work first." Akmed then grabbed his pistol from the table he was cleaning and smiled while walking to the door. "I should be back in about an hour."

"Meanwhile Anand, I need you to go online at the desk and find out what a **Tong** is." Kintu then picked up his cell phone and dialed Nafy's cell number one more time.

"Nafy…where are you?" Anand's eyes opened wide.

I'm at my uncle's house. Is Anand there?

"Yes…he is here," said Kintu. Then he handed Anand the cell phone.

"Are you alright…did they harm you?"

I'm fine.

"How did you escape?"

I called my uncle not Kintu and he sent his men. They beat the shit out of those guards.

"What men?"

He doesn't only sell goats.

"I wondered how your father could afford that big house."

"Give me the phone." Kintu grabbed the phone from Anand. "Nafy I need you to stay where you are."

"No, I want to be with Anand."

"We have to settle all debts with the Egyptians before it is safe. I'll call you when that happens." Kintu then hung up and pulled the battery out of the cell phone.

"Why didn't you let me finish talking to her?"

"The phone can be tracked in about one to five minutes," said Kintu while holding his sore ribs. "I'll put the battery back in later." Anand walked over to the computer a little mad at his brother. He then searched *Egyptian Tongs*.

"That faggot-ass Egyptian king wants to curl his hair," said Anand as he carried the laptop to Kintu's bed. He knew the king was Nubian and already had curly nappy hair.

Bronze Hair Curling and Cutting Tongs
575 BC to 1194 BC

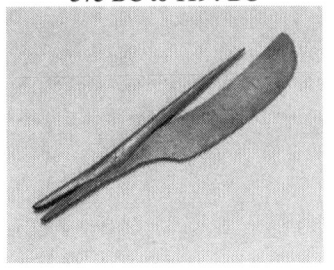

"Where would this be in King Piankhi's tomb?" asked Kintu.

"The priests buried everything the king needed in the after-life," said Anand. "Even these to trim his Afro." Kintu smiled.

"I have a friend that works at the museum," said Kintu. "But he won't be back in town until his pilgrimage to Mecca (Hajj) has ended."

"When will that be?"

"He should be back before November 9th when the Hajj ends."

"That's three days from now." Anand became agitated and scared knowing he needed Akhenaten's help from being eaten alive. "I need a ride to the museum. The museum director knew dad and knows we donated King Piye. He will let me view the sarcophagus."

"The museum's being guarded by the police," said Kintu while trying to sit up in the bed.

"If they are Sudanese, they will let me in."

"And how will you get that stone sarcophagus open? You can't do it alone."

"The museum has tools to open it," said Anand while grabbing Kintu's cell phone and battery. "I'm calling a *Careem* (Sudan Uber) to pick me up a block away from here."

"Grab some cash from my wallet and if you need help," said Kintu. "Speed dial the number two on the cell and Akmed will answer."

"I will be back shortly with the artifact."

Anand made it to the museum and met with the curator who was excited to meet him. Later in his office with a cash bribe, and minutes of explaining his situation about the Egyptians, the curator agreed to let Anand search the sarcophagus for the artifact. But only after the museum closed at lunch time for its midday cleaning and after the janitors left.

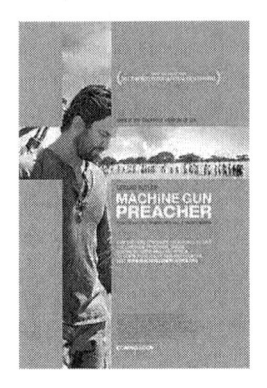

Anand was told to return around 12:30 pm so he walked from the museum to the *Friendship* theater which was a block away. He wanted to see the hit 2011 movie *Machine Gun Preacher*, about a former biker gang member that protects a southern Sudenese orphange.

When the movie was over, he called Akmed for a pickup while walking back toward the museum.

Chapter 5

The trip

It was a little past noon time and the sun seemed low in the sky as the city of Khartoum's air became visible. Anand didn't know he was being followed as he got closer to the museum. The curator let him in the museum with a fake smile on his face. "I told the janitors to leave early and the Secret Police will be back from lunch in twenty minutes."

"This may only take ten," lied Anand not really knowing.

"Your father was an honorable man and donated money to keep this museum open."

"Yes he was," said Anand as the curator grabbed the special tools for opening the sarcophagus as he stood by. It took both men's strength to open the lid and slide it onto a special wheeled table.

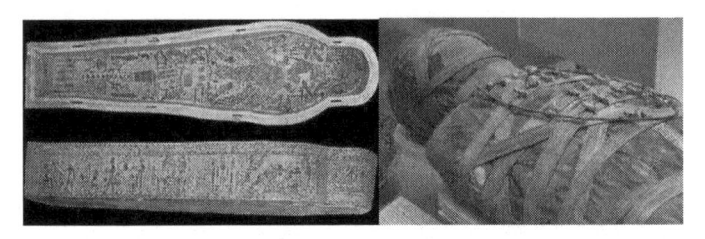

Anand didn't know where the **Tong** was so he began to feel along the mummy's skull hoping the cutters were close to the head. Then he saw an opening as the wrappings were laying open along the waistline. The curator became scared as he stared continuously at his watch. Anand then reached into the mummy and only found one artifact.

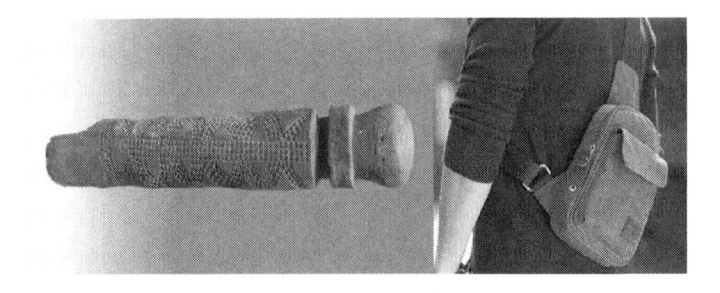

"Good, lets close it up," said Anand as he placed the Tong in the sachel and then they closed the sarcophagus. The curator was relieved as Anand walked quickly to the restroom.

Akmed was two blocks away when Anand exited the museum. He spotted the car as he heard wheels braking to a screeching stop. A black vehicle pulled up in front of him as two men had guns drawn. "Get in Mr. Abbul." They shoved him into the back seat and sped away as Akmed began to follow. The black car turned on Tirhaqa Street as Akmed never lost sight of them. The car then made a hard left turn and drove right into an open gate of the *Embassy of the Arab Republic of Egypt.*

I'm fucked again. Thought Anand while contemplating whether he should piss on himself. They took his cell phone and the sachel as they escorted him to an interrogation room, pushing him onto an unpadded steel chair. "Don't take too long or I'm leaving a surprise."

"Just sit quietly," said one agent as he slammed the metal door shut. Anand looked up at the camera in the corner of the room and flipped it the bird.

Two minutes later as Anand was deciding to piss himself, the door swung open with two different agents entering, one fat and one skinny.

"Mr. Abbul, I want you to think very clearly and try to remember these faces," said the skinny agent in Arabic. He threw a folder open with old survellance photos of King Tut in 1969.

He had a afro in one picture while standing across the street in Chicago near a *Black Panther* safe house. He was watching a police raid that ended in multiple shots fired.

"That's King…I mean…a man I met in Egypt."

"We know it's King Tutankhamun."

"He look's like the first Lionel from the Jeffersons," said Anand.

"Who?"

"I mean…what's he doing in America?"

"We believe he is manipulating history to flow in a direction he wants."

"That's crazy," said Anand. "If he is doing that, he would have to know the future."

"Not necessarily."

"Your telling me?" asked Anand. "Throughtout history, he has been steering it in the direction he wants?"

The fat agent leaned toward him. "We are asking you Mr. Abbul…what is he trying to accomplish?"

"How the hell do I know? I just helped him because he knew where my king was buried."

"Who bombed the Giza Pyramid?"

"It exploded from the inside," lied Anand knowing it was the Americans.

"How?"

"All I know is, he was entering the pyramid to find a way home. He must of set off an internal self destruct bomb."

"We have one more picture." The skinny agent reached into his suit's chest pocket and threw two photos on the interrogation table. It was pictures of King Tut next to Anand's dad Timbuku. One was in France marked February and the other in Buenos Aires, May of 1982.

Obelisco/ Plaza de la Republica

"That's more than one picture…and what's this?" asked Anand.

"Your dad was seen talking to Tutankhamun more than once in the mid-eighties. This confirms he is not aging and has been at the scene of major events in history. We want to know why?"

"Like I said," shouted Anand not knowing his dad visited Argentina. "He helped me find King Piankhi's mummy."

"Why did you steal the ankh from Germany?"

"Ok…King Tut wanted it in exchange for getting my king back."

"Why?"

"I don't know and don't care."

"We do know he is looking for you and your wife."

"I know."

"Then why are you walking out in public?"

"I am tired of hiding." The two gents just stared at him, contemplating whether he was lying. They left the room and returned two minutes later.

"You are free to leave," said the fat agent as he threw Anand's cell phone and sachel on the table.

"Oh no…I need a ride."

"Sure, around the corner where we picked you up at."

"I'll just call a Careem." (Uber)

Anand walked out of the Egyptian Embassy and Akmed was waiting in his car for him.

"I am glad to see you."

"What did they want?" asked Ankmed.

"They asked me questions about King Piye and why my dad was in Argentina before the Falkland War started."

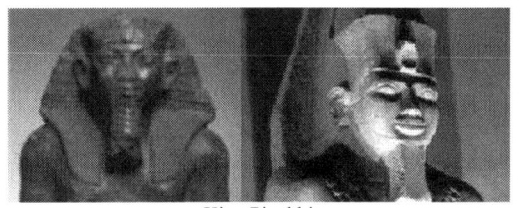

King Piankhi

"Did they ask you why King Tut was there?"

"How did you know that?"

"Because I am taking you to him," said Akmed while aiming a gun, low and out of sight. "Get in."

"You are my brother's best friend and now you are betraying him." Akmed began driving fast while placing the gun in his lap.

"You have a ransom on your head and the money will help me and my wife leave this country forever."

"You are a sell out like that coon Steve Harvey?"

"Who?"

"I'm not going anywhere," said Anand as he grabbed the door handle on his side of the car. He opened the door and fell out, rolling on the ground while moaning like a pornstar. He was bruised as Akmed tried to stop with three cars behind him. Anand jumped to his feet and began limping.

He walked into the Kush Café while dialing his cell phone. "Brother, it's me...your friend Akmed tried to kidnap me."

"Why?"

"For the ransom. He pulled a gun on me, but I escaped."

"Where are you now?"

"At the Kush Café, three blocks south of the museum."

"Did you get the artifact?"

"Yes."

"I'm heading to the Al Mashtal hotel."

"Wait there, I will send my wife to pick you up."

Anand reached the hotel, but waited at the *Love-Box* souveneir shop across the street. He was smart because Akmed drove up three minutes later with two other men. He knew then Kintu's phone was being tapped. He waited till they left and caught a *Tirhal* yellow taxi that was parked in front of the hotel.

The taxi was one block from the safehouse when it skidded to a stop in front of a parked black van.

"Not again," said Anand. "Is this whole damn city trying to kidnap me?" He remained silent as two men from the van with guns opened the taxi door. They pulled him out as the van's back door was opened.

"You better have plastic on those seats."

"Shut the fuck up," said the kidnapper, handcuffing Anand's hands in the back and then pushing him in the van. The other man paid the taxi driver 100 dollars in Egytian money.

There was a sheet of plastic duct tape to the floor of the van and Anand smiled.

"I see the word is spreading," he said with a smile.

"Your day's of shitting in cars is over," said the driver.

They drove down Army Road and then over the Victory Bridge. After a couple of turns, they headed north on Libya Street. Anand knew they were heading to Egypt.

A few hours after only stopping to eat, Anand thought about pissing his pants before reaching Lake Nubia which was in southern Egypt.

"Are we going swimming?" asked Anand.

"Where you're going, you will be swimming in boiling vegetable oil."

"Oh damn," whispered Anand. He became quiet after that statement and knew he had to escape somehow.

They reached the Naj Kibdi peer as a mid-size boat awaited to take them to the Seti Hotel. There they would catch a flight out of Abu Sibel Airport.

They sailed north to an abandoned peer, to an awaiting mid-size Toyota. They drove past the Abu Sibel temple which was moved to higher grounds in 1968 at a cost of 40 million dollars (True). It would have been flooded because the Aswan Dam was built and completed in July 1970.

"Do you guys know King Ramsees II was Nubian?" asked Anand as the van became silent. "It is believed that he chased Moses out of Egypt...but he didn't."

"Stop your lies!" yelled the driver. "Look at the face carvings...they are not Kush."

"The original head had a large Nubian nose. That face was replaced when the temple was moved to higher ground."

1968   1905

"One more false word out of your mouth and we are going to tape it shut."

"His DNA Haplogroup was E1B1A," said Anand knowing his mouth was about to be duct-taped. "He was the same race as Moses and the Hebrew slaves...and they were not white or beige like you guys."

The van skidded to a stop as the kidnapper on the passenger side removed a roll of duct-tape from the glove-box.

"Your lying ass is going to be quiet until you meet the prince."

"Are you talking about King Fuck...I mean King Tut? Technically he is Prince Tut."

The kidnappers force a old camel burger wrapping of paper into Anand's mouth and then tightly duct taped his mouth. He just moaned as loud as he could. *Your momma eats monkey balls.* The kidnappers didn't understand his words.

Chapter 6

The long flights

The Toyota van drove to the Sibel airport and Anand was forced on a private plane that flew low and northward along the Nile River. They landed under the cover of night at the Sphinx Airport that was north-east of Cairo.

Anand's mouth was still taped shut as the two kidnappers walked him off the tarmac to an awaiting black limo.

He was sure King Tut was in the car as the men removed the handcuffs, duct tape, and the ball of wrappings in his mouth.

"I'm going to shit all over those seats."

"I don't think you will," said one kidnapper. Anand was pushed into the limo and his mouth opened in shock. He sat back in the seat and whispered two words.

"Oh shit."

"I should kill you now for putting my daughter in danger." It was Nafy's dad and he was angry. "Did you think you could take her to America without me knowing?" he said while leaning toward him.

"Nafy is safe with her uncle," said Anand.

"My brother was beaten almost to death and she was kidnapped again by Tut's men. If you love her...man up and do the right thing. You are going on a long flight and I was told that all he wants is that thing you have shoved up your ass. You are to take a flight and smuggle it through customs. When he get's it, he will let my daughter go."

"How do you know I have the artifact?"

"The satchel was empty and your brother told Akmed...you have a history of shoving things up your ass."

"That snitch."

"Just deliver it and get my daughter back."

"I guess I have no choice," said Anand.

"No you don't. Tut likes you, that's why he helped you find our King Piye...even though you blew up the Giza with him in it."

"He lied to me and said he was contacting an invasion fleet to take over the world."

"That pyramid wasn't contacting anyone in space. Tut's men said it was only transfering energy to power Atlantis. I think that's where you are going."

Nobody's eating my ass out. Thought Anand believing Nafy was still safe and he was being delivered for dinner. He decided to escape at the first chance he got.

"Tut has my daughter and won't release her until he sees you face-to-face. Be cooperative and have a nice trip."

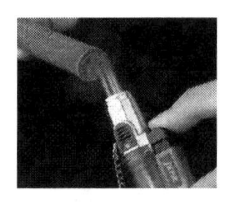

Nafy's dad lit his cigar and then tapped his lighter on the limo window. The door swung open. "Call me when he is on the flight."

"Yes sir," said one of the kidnappers as he pulled Anand out of the Limo. He then felt that lamb Gyro with Tzatziki sauce begin to run through his system, moving closer and closer to his butt hole. With the Tong up his ass, he knew how a San-Fran Gay man felt that had to take a shit in the middle of being fucked.

I wonder if Akhenaten lied to me and is working with his son Tutankhamen. Anand then began thinking about that big knuckle Ethiopian henchman. *They all maybe trying to manipulate me in getting the Tong and being on their dinner table at the same time?*

Anand was driven behind Almaza Airbase to the Le Passage hotel. It was the cheapest hotel closest to the Cairo International Airport. The two men already had a room and Anand knew it was his only chance to escape. He was pushed into the hotel room that had a new winter coat on the bed and one large suitcase.

"Is that my luggage?"

"Yes, the one you were taking to America."

"I would give you two a kiss, but you smell as bad as I do…only naturally."

"Get in the shower and wash your ass…your plane leaves in two hours."

Anand entered the bathroom, pulled the artifact out of his ass, and then took a well needed shit. He stepped into the shower and stood under the hot water for two minutes before deciding to jerk off. *I miss my wife.* He thought with his dick in his hand.

He finished showering and decided when they entered the airport, he was going to run to the nearest armed police officer.

An hour later, as they entered the Cairo International Airport, Anand was forced to carry his luggage as his captor's walked closely behind him, one carrying the winter coat. He was anxious as he scanned the baggage check-in area for any security guard.

"Don't try anything funny or we will beat you to the ground."

"Where are we going?"

"You're flying to England alone…we are just making sure you get on the flight."

"No problem," said Anand as he saw a guard near the check-in counter. All three men were about to get in line when Anand dropped the luggage and ran toward the armed security guard.

"Help!" he yelled to the officer. He was out of breath quickly as the men chased him. He reached the guard while pointing behind him. "Those men kidnapped me."

"No…they didn't Mr. Abbul," said the guard while holding Anand's arm. "You are getting on that flight."

"How do you know my name?"

"Thanks Rasheed," said one captor.

"Is this whole damn country after my head?"

"Only the prince," said the other captor. "You are a famous man in Egypt." Anand looked all around the airport for any most-wanted posters.

"How does everybody know my face?"

"Just shut your mouth."

Anand was put on the seven hour flight to London England and all the flight attendants knew who he was. He asked, but they did not tell him how they knew his name. They just gave him an angry stare every time they walked passed him. He knew he had a better chance of escaping in London as the plane landed on a cold rainy day.

He exited the ramp and two large white men and a Customs police officer were waiting for him. They looked like famous dead wrestlers on steroids.

The officer grabbed Anand's hands and handcuffed them. "We heard you tried to escape in Cairo," said the Customs officer. "That's not happening here."

"You don't have to do this. It's embarrassing."

"You're a black man in this country," said the officer. "Local white citizens are use to Arabs being arrested."

"You forgot profiled first."

"We are going on a special flight with you this time," said one of the wrestlers.

"Where are we going?" asked Anand.

"You don't have to worry about that," said the other.

All four men walked to the other side of the airport and twenty minutes later, got on a 737 SAS Scandinavian aircraft that was almost empty. They took off as soon as all three men were seated and flew north for 15 hours to Svalbard, a land mass that's part of Norway and the midway point to the North Pole. It is also the location of the *Dooms Day Vault* with fifty thousand various seeds from all over the world.

After returning from the airplane restroom and cleaning the itchy **Tong** that was in his ass, Anand sat at his window seat and then stared at the blonde Norwegian across the aisle from him.

"Tell me one thing?" asked Anand. The guard just sat quietly with his eyes closed. "Are we going to the North Pole to see that fat man in the red suit?" The Norwegian smiled as Anand leaned into the window seeing ocean and then snow covered mountains in the distance.

"Do you want to know why we are heading north?" asked the blonde Norwegian.

"I know one thing…that baldhead King Tut and his family don't like the cold."

"We are getting off this flight but you are flying north to Argentina."

"Shouldn't we be heading southwest?"

"Have you really taken a good looked at the United Nations flag?"

"No."

"That flag is a real map of the earth. The shortest distance to South America and being able to refuel is to fly through Canada and then the United States."

"I read about this on YouTube," said Anand. "So what you're saying is…the earth is flat?"

"When you left Egypt, you couldn't fly directly to South America. It's too far. The shortest distance is north then west."

"You're full of shit," said Anand. "The earth is shaped like an egg…that's why it's too far to fly along the equator."

"No…that's what they want you to believe. Ask any soldier that's flown from America to Japan. They all have to stop in Alaska first.

It's a refueling stop and planes fly in a straight line to get to the Far East.

"Bull-shit."

"When you hold a cup of water…it is level. Water on a calm lake is level, and when you fly high over the ocean, the water looks level.

Hangzhou Bridge, China / 249 miles long

"The entire world has been told the Earth curves eight inches for every mile (1.6 Kilometers). It's a lie, but since people have had a globe shoved into their faces since pre-school, they accept it."

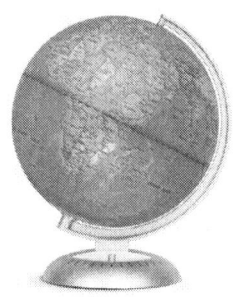

"Or like me," said Anand. "I don't give a shit."

"If the entire world believed the earth is flat, they would try to find the end."

"Tell me this isn't why nobody's allowed to visit Antarctica?" asked Anand.

"Yes and no?"

"What's down there?"

"Quiet Hanz," said the brunette Norwegian "You've said enough."

Before the plane landed, Anand was given the winter coat and when the aircraft door was opened, a crisp winter breeze was felt throughout the airplane.

A yellow portable stair ramp was driven up to the plane and the pilots exited first. Anand unconsciously decided to run and escape from the two guards. He ran down the stairs onto the tarmac and slid in the fresh fallen snow to a mouth opening stop. "Amun Ra Sekhmet," Anand whispered hoping the words would somehow save him. All it did was vibrate the **Tong** in his ass. The two Norwegians laughed as they exited the plane.

There was only one tower, four aircraft hangars, and a small concourse.

Anand turned 360 degrees and saw nothing but snow and mountains. *I'm in white hell.* He thought looking at his escorts. He then followed the pilots into the waiting area of the building. The Norwegians caught up to him, smiling. "Where were you going?"

"I had to go to the restroom," lied Anand.

"Your next plane is arriving in two hours. We suggest you get on it because if you miss it you will be sleeping with *Customs* until the next flight arrives."

"And when would that be?" asked Anand.

"In seven days."

"Here's your ticket," said the blonde Norwegian while handing it to him. Anand looked at the arrival destination. *Where the fuck is Etah Greenland?* He thought seeing it was a connecting flight from Qaanaaq Airport which was 75 miles away (120 Km).

Anand didn't know it was an abandoned town and he was booked on a helicopter flight with two Canadian archaeologists.

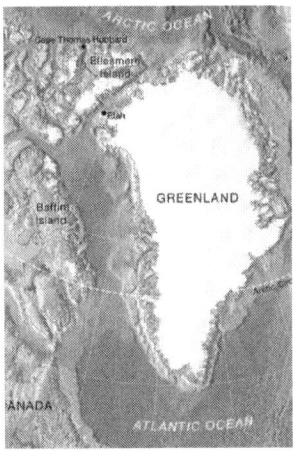

It took Anand's flight almost a whole day to reach Greenland. After refueling at an unknown stop and finally landing in Quaanaaq, he was met by an Egyptian man with a large guard that was to escort him onto the helicopter.

"Mr. Abbul, my name is Khaleef and we will be accompanying you to Etah."

"I thought I was going to Canada and then Argentina. Why are we going to Etah?"

"You are in no position to ask questions."

"You better tell me where I'm going or I will lose you like a blind tour guide."

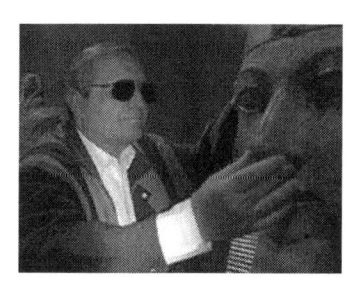

"If you do…you will never see your wife again." Anand began to walk away.

"Mr. Abbul…I have a recording of your wife." He then pressed the video play buttom on his cell phone and held it up.

My love I am ok. Just do what they say. Tut promised me he wasn't going to eat you.

"Ok," said Anand as he began to smile, recognizing the face of the black male Canadian scientist.

What the hell is my college roommate doing here? Then the ugly female scientist turned toward him.

"I'm Dr. Celeste...Gertrude Celeste and this here is my new assistant Jamal Lewis."

"How you doing," said Jamal as he shook Anand's hand and then Khaleef.

Dr. Celeste walked ahead of the Egyptian as Anand began to giggle at the woman's fucked up teeth. He felt a little better as they walked closer to the helicopter. *Tyrone better not get us killed.*

Chapter 7

Operation High Jump

Anand lost track of time as he sat next to the smelly Egyptian on the first row of cramped seats.

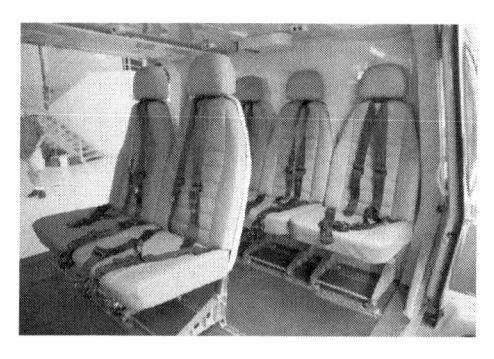

The helicopter vibrated continuously which kept him from sleeping. He was then startled by a violent wind gust caused by the Aurora Borealis that made the helicopter decreased it's altitude before landing. Dr. Celeste became excited as they landed at an abandoned town on the shoreline of Etah.

It was a clear day but cold as the scientist began removing their luggage and equipment. Anand followed Khaleef as the guard followed him. They waited near Dr. Celeste as the helicopter was on standby with its blades still turning. A large smoky vehicle had come into their view from a hill-top as the female turned toward Khaleef.

"Mr. Ammun, the Queen has agreed to his terms." Khaleef then opened his briefcase that was some-kind of satellite tranmitting device with one green and one red button. She then pressed the green button.

"The prince will be pleased. You have made a wise decision." The helicopter then took off, electronically knowing both archeolgist were staying. The truck pulled up as another pale-face Egyptian exited and began loading their luggage and equipment. Anand couldn't help himself and asked one more time.

"Where are we going?"

Khaleef turned to Anand as they all closed the doors of the truck. "Have you heard of the U.S. Naval explorer Admiral Byrd?"

"I read about him in college."

"There was a reason...or rather an excuse he used this town in order to explore the North Pole."

"What excuse?" asked Anand as Khaleef paused in thought.

"History has recorded that he explored the North Pole, but in actuality at first, he found several dead Emperor penguins in a metal lined fish-nets on the shores of Etah Greenland in 1926.

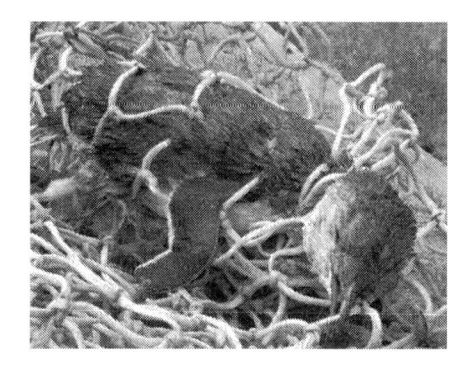

He knew those penguins only existed at the South Pole. He did an investigation and discovered one of our magnectic rail tunnels had broken apart because of an earthquake.

One of his scuba divers was sent down and accidently sucked in by his metal helmet. He was later found four hours later floating in the ocean by a fishing boat near King George Island. "

"In England?" asked Anand.

"No south of the Falkland Islands," said Khaleef. "Close to the South pole."

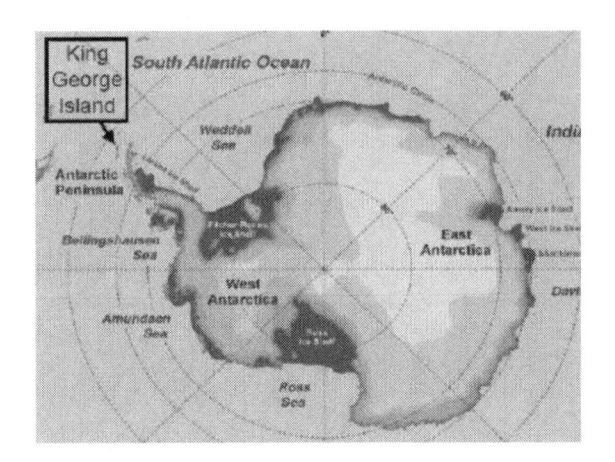

"Was he alive?"

"Yes, but he later died...suspiciously after trying to contact the NBC Radio Network."

"Hanz and Franz told me the Earth is flat."

"Who?"

"Forget them...so what you're saying is the positive attraction of the North Pole repulses metals like when two positive magnectic fields of a magnet are pushed together?"

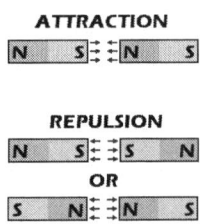

"Yes, transporting metal at a continuous high rate of speed."

"Are you charging Canada a toll fee?"

"No...England," said the Egyptian. "They again can travel to-and-from London to Argentina in three hours instead of fifteen."

"So that's how the British won the war in the Falklands," stated Anand. "I saw a picture of Tutankhamen in Buenos Aires taken in 1982."

"We transported British troops to Port San Carlos," said Khaleef, not saying the Germans knew and tried in 1938 to find the transport tunnels.

They temporarily claim Antarctica land they called New Swabia and tried to set up a military base.

Operation High Jump

"I remember Admiral Byrd commanding an naval armada in 1946 down to the Antarctica on an armed expedition," said Anand as the truck left the small town toward a large mountain crevice.

"It was rumored the Germans escaped there after the war," said Jamal. "Alot of their submarines were unaccounted for."

"They were looking for Germans and found us," said Khaleef. "They fought valiantly for one point five hours and retreated as one of their planes got lost due to the cold temperature. It flew the wrong way too long and crashed."

"I thought the Germans shot it down?" asked Anand.

"No one shot it down," said Khaleef. "It flew into the wall."

"What wall?" asked Anand.

"God's wall," said Jamal as the truck stopped in front of a large ice door with exposed gears.

"How do you know it's a wall?" asked Anand. "And...are you talking about the firmament?"

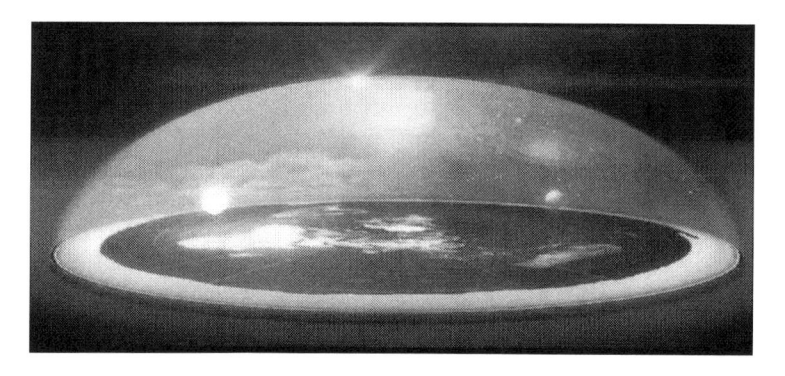

"Yes", said Dr. Celeste. "We are living in a snow globe. Have you read the bible?"

"I'm Muslim," said Anand. "But I did think that rocket scientist Von Braun's tombstone was strange."

Psalms 19:1 The heavens declare the glory of God; and the firmament sheth his handy work.

"He knew and had to keep it a secret," said Jamal. "Why do you see all rockets curve when taking off? They have too or they'll crash into the dome."

"And have you notice that all trees grow only straight up (vertically) on all hills?" asked Dr. Celeste.

"I never really paid attention to that," said Jamal. "Why?"

"They say gravity, but I also believe Jesus was white with sun-tan lotion…in hot ass Israel."

"The whole world doesn't care," said Anand. "Including me."

"Nasa has the flat earth flight path showing in plain site," said Jamal. "Rockets fly in a straight direction during takeoff. Magnectic and low gravity fields maintain its altitude in a low earth orbit. On the flat Earth map, the International Space Station flies over the Earth in a circular egg shape pattern."

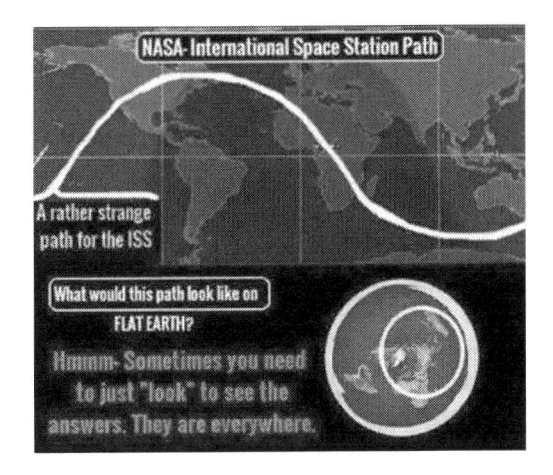

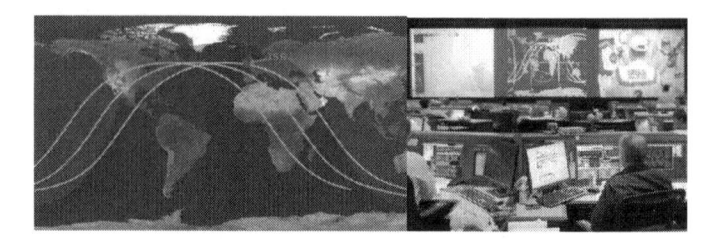

"There are no real pictures of the entire Earth," said Dr. Celeste. "Just computer generated composites."

"And why haven't the Americans gone back to the moon?" asked Anand.

"Because they never went," said Jamal. "That's why they try to shift the focus on Mars, especially with that Utah desert dirt."

Who took this picture? Maybe a Martian.

"You are right Ty...I mean Dr. Lewis. And the Van Allen Radiation Belt would've killed the astronauts."

"Mr. Abbul," interrupted Khaleef. "Have you heard of the Mandela Effect?"

"No, what is it?"

"It is changes in the timeline where people are aware that events have changed in the past that they remembered differently."

"My wife said...before we were married she remembered there was never a Giza Solar Boat Museum."

"There wasn't," said Khaleef. "And the alignment of the stars with the Giza pyramid and Orion's Belt also changed."

"I'm not an astronomer, but how?"

"The Americans believe it was the Cern particle accelerator in Geneva, Switzerland that changed our time-line."

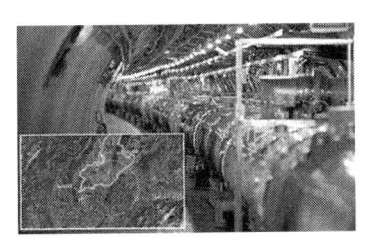

"What really caused the changes?" asked Anand. "King Tut?"

"No…it was God," said Dr. Celeste.

"Why?"

"Maybe to prove to the unbelievers that he exist," said Jamal.

The large ice door began to open as Khaleef hung up his cell phone that had no signal. There was a large main tunnel with cable wires along the sides. They walked through the tunnel to a smaller entrance as a guard waited at the door of a transport vehicle marked with the faded number (2) on the side.

They all entered the vehicle and the scientist stored their equipment into secured lockers at the back of the transport. Everyone sat and strapped into facing seats that were old like 1950's locomotive trains.

A red light then turned green as the transport began to slowly move at an increasing speed. Khaleef looked over at Anand and he could see the fear in his eyes.

"Mr. Abbul…you don't have to worry about being eaten. The prince only wants the Tong."

"I don't have a Tong."

"We know it's up your ass." Dr. Celeste started smiling.

"How did you know?" asked Anand.

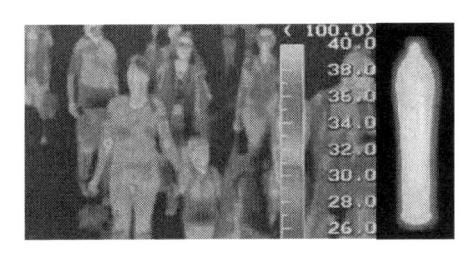

"International law requires all airports to have body thermal scanners to find sick passengers," said Khaleef. "Your ass lit up like a glow stick."

"I can't wait to get it out," said Anand.

"The Prince has ordered us not to remove it."

"Why?" asked Anand.

"I don't know," smiled Khaleef. "And I'm glad."

The transport then slowed its speed and came to slow stop. Then it veered to the right into another tunnel and increased its speed again. Anand began to panick thinking that anything that obstructed the tunnel like a baseball size rock, would kill everybody in seconds. He began to sweat in fear as Khaleef stared at him with a calm look.

"Mr. Abbul I assure you this transport is safe. We send empty test transports everyday to assure the tunnels are clear." Anand began to calm down, not knowing it was the Tong that was affecting his boby to change moods.

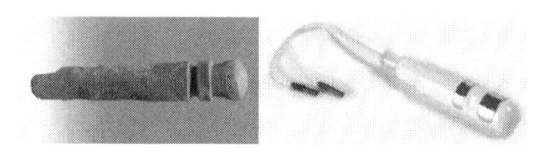

Khaleef knew this because the Tong was not just a rock carving. Embedded in its interior was a high tech cellular synaptic transferer. It was hidden in King Piankhi's mummy when the *Assyrians invaded Egypt that was ruled by the Nubians in 676 B.C.* (True). Then a cold weather climate-change killed farms combined with low rainfall. Egypt was cursed, some believed because of the enslavement of so-called black Hebrews that built their cities. The local population slowly declined as many fled the country in order to survive.

Chapter 8

Surrender

Two hours later the transport stopped at a station with a sign that indicated Pakistan in four different languages; Arabic, English, Spanish and Chinese. There was an old sign written in Greek that was barely noticeable as Anand then knew how **Alexander the Great** conquered most of the world. *That faggot cheated.* Thought Anand wondering how they transported horses.

Anand then stood up to go use the restroom in the rear. He was hoping to somehow escape in a country that spoke his first language. Unfortunately there were no windows in the restroom as he pissed with a frown on his face. He returned to his seat walking past his friend and the fake British yuck-mouth archaeological spy.

"How many times have you two been on these transports?" asked Anand.

"We are not aloud to say," said Dr. Celeste.

"It's my first time too," said Anand while looking over at Khaleef. "Does this train go to Egypt?"

"Yes…it can," he said unbelievably.

"Then why did you have me fly all the way to the North Pole to ride this speeding coffin back down to the south."

"The Tong in your ass is repowered by the northern magnectic fields produced by the Aurora-borealis you flew through in Greenland."

"Are you saying I got a powered piece of equipment up my ass?"

"Yes." Anand jumped up. "I have to take a shit." He ran to the restroom a little worried. Three minutes later Anand returned feeling relieved while sitting sluggishly.

"Where's the Tong?" asked Khaleef.

"I put it back."

"Disgusting," whispered the female scientist.

The transport sped south from Pakistan to a unknown island nation call Mauritus which was west of the bottom of Africa. It stopped under the resort capital of Port Louis.

The transport stopped as two tall men entered. Anand was frightened because one of the men looked like Canuk. They walked toward the back of the transport as Jamal jumped up and punched the guard in the face. He then grabbed Anand's arm, forcing him to get up and run for the door. The two men then ran to an upward staircase next to a elevator as the transport doors closed.

"Where are we going?" asked Anand as he was out of breath and almost stopping.

"Keep moving," said Tyrone. "I have a tracking device in me and the CIA will authorize a flight for us."

"How do you know they have a airport here?"

"If they don't…we'll charter a boat. Or do you want go back?"

"No…those bastards are sexual perverts and really greedy." *For human flesh.*

"They were going to eat you and I voluteered to save you."

"You do owe me one," said Anand. "That infectious hooker was going to let you fuck her raw." Tyrone smiled.

"I was so drunk that night, I would've fucked her pimp."

"I always thought you were a homo."

The men ran up the stairs for twenty minutes before reaching the surface of the island.

"I am…fucking…exausted," said Anand out of breath. "My college legs are gone."

Tyrone slowly opened a hall door while pulling a gun from his ankle holster.

"How did you get that through customs?"

"Quiet," whisper Tyrone as he heard guards talking about eating an endangered Mauritus Fruit Bat smothered in onions. *Haven't those fuckers heard of the Corona Virus?* Anand asked himself.

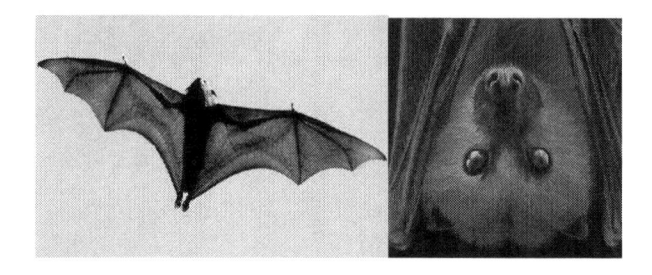

The guards walked by and Tyrone signaled Anand to follow him through a marked alley exit door that closed automatically.

They ran onto a busy downtown Port Louis street and luckily found a tourist pay phone near a souveneir shop. Tyrone called the U.S. Embassy and was instructed to go directly to the airport. He hailed a taxi and both men sluggishly fell into the back seat. "Do you have money to pay for this ride?" asked Anand.

"They use Indian Rupee," said Tyrone. "But American cash is excepted here."

"I have 200 pounds."

"Keep it."

Twenty minutes later as Anand awakened from a nap in the cab. They reached the airport and quickly walked in. Tyrone used an airport customer service phone and five minutes later, a airport ticket manager escorted them to the concourse of a recently boarded Air Maritius flight going to Cape Town South Africa.

"I'm glad you still have the Tong," said Tyrone. "It's going to have some leverage in negotiating our demands to the Atlantians."

"I don't have the Tong."

"What!"

"I hid it on the transport when Khaleef said it was electrical."

"We…I mean you have to go back."

"I'm not going back. I look tender and delicious to those fuckers."

"We need the Tong."

"I don't need it."

"What about Nafy?"

"Okay," whined Anand.

The men left the airport and took another taxi to the U.S. Embassy. Anand was injected with a tracking chip into his left scrotum.

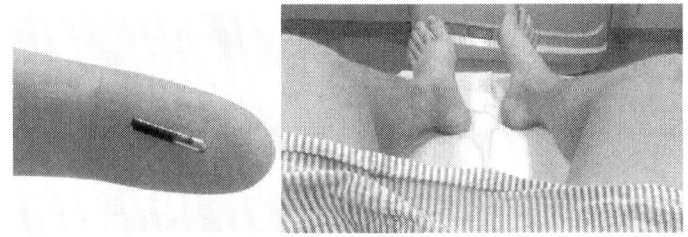

He was then driven near the street close to the brick building's secret transport alley exit door.

Anand walked the street like a Jersey hooker, back and forth, hoping to get recaptured. For 40 minutes he walked and almost gave up, when a car drove up next to him and two Chinese men pulled him into the back seat. They drove away quickly as Anand knew they were not King Tut's men.

"I'm definitely hungry for some Chinese food...now that you guys showed up. Do you two speak English?"

"Quiet!" yelled the driver. The kidnapper to his left then punched Anand in his ribs. He hunched over in pain as the car drove into the back of the *Happy Dragon Restaurant* in the middle of China-town. Anand was pulled out the car and forced to walk through the kitchen.

He was then pushed down a flight of basement stairs. As the men walked passed numerous paper boxes to a set of double doors, Anand was curious as to what was on the other side. The doors swung open and his curiosity was answered. It was Canuk standing behind Khaleef. He had two metal braces close to his knee-caps as he smiled at first and then a look of anger fell upon his face.

"Mr. Abbul, it is good to see you again."

"The feeling isn't mutual."

"The Prince is very upset that you escaped and flew a familiar face here to make sure you don't try anything again."

"Hello Canuk. I see you got your legs reattached."

"He has orders to take a non-lethal bite out of you…if you try to escape again."

"I'm not," said Anand. *He looks hungry.*

"Do you still have the Tong?"

"Yes," lied Anand.

"Good, then we are continuing our journey."

"I like this country."

"You can come back if the Prince decides to let you go."

"Oh he will," said Anand as he noticed Canuk seemed a little shorter.

The three of them returned to the same brick wall as the Chinese men assured them the street was empty before opening the secret brick door that led to the magnetic train. Anand was glad to see it was the same number (2) transport as he dreaded sticking that Tong back up his ass.

They all strapped into their seats as Anand was mentally preparing himself for another history lesson. Ten minutes later after returning from the restroom, Khaleef opened his mouth towards him.

Her we go. Thought Anand while feeling pressure on his colon. *Did that thing grow?*

"Mr. Abbul, that stunt you pulled with the Canadian scientist has cost us some precious time."

"I just wanted to see the country side of the island."

"That Canadian CIA agent almost cost you your life." Khaleef then reached into his suit chest pocket. "I have a text that Agent Tyrone Johnson attended the same university you attended. Am I assuming you knew this individual?"

"Yes," said Anand. "He was my roomate during my first semester in college."

"He was sent by the Pentagon to locate the so-called Lost City of Atlantis," said Khaleef. "Except it is not lost."

"I assume it's somewhere in the Antarctica?" asked Anand.

"Yes, except it is in the control of our Prince."

"I thought Tut wanted to awaken his parents?" asked Anand a little confused "That's why he needed the ankh."

"He only awakened his two mother's," said Khaleef. "King Akhenaten was already awake. King Tut was only luring his father away from Atlantis to reunite him with his wives in order to takeover it."

"Pussy has that affect on the weak minded," whispered Anand.

"King Akhenaten needs the Tong to reclaim Atlantis."

"He looked sick," said Anand. "Almost like a cancer patient."

"It is only temporary," said Khaleef. "Let me tell you another story."

"Please don't."

"Have you heard of Ribeiroia?"

"No."

"Ribeiroia is a parasite in America that infects fresh water snails. This parasite in egg form is released and infects the tadpoles of frogs."

"I'm an archaelogist not a biologist."

"There's a lesson in this story. The parasite attaches and causes the frog to grow three legs, hindering the amphibian to hop away from predators. Birds eat the frogs and the parasites grow to full term releasing eggs in the birds stomach and then is shitted most of the time back into a lake or pond."

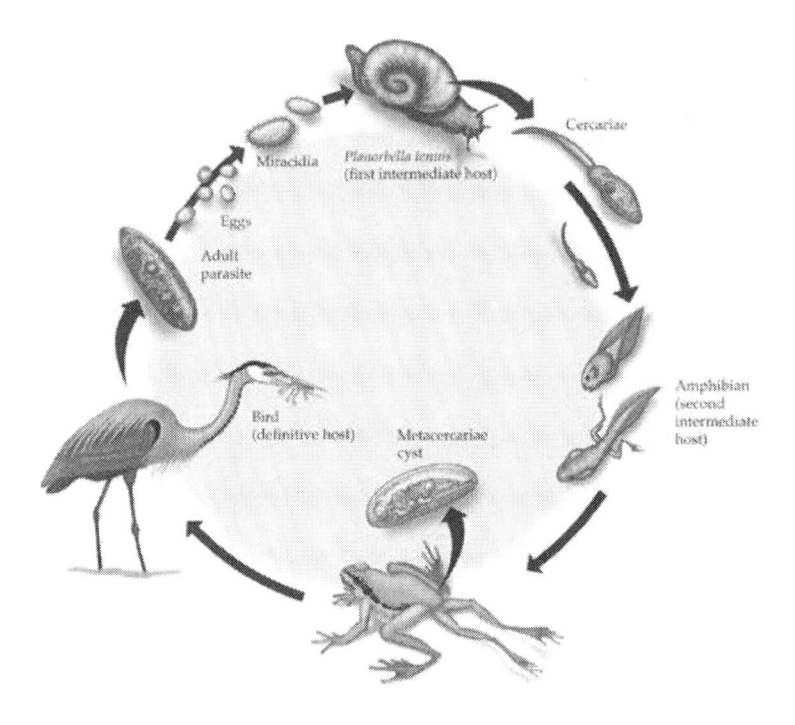

"Why are you telling me this?"

"King Akhenaken needs the Tong to complete this process in order to live."

"Are you telling me they are all clones?"

"Kind of…the process is done like the Cicada insect in Alabama that hatches only every 13 years."

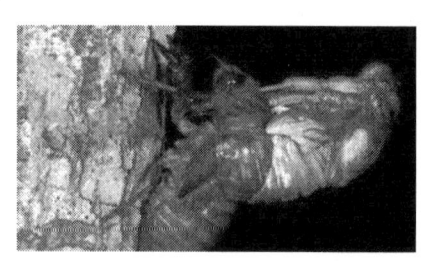

"I'm afraid to ask how are the Atlantians hatched?"

"Last year when you helped free the women from their tombs, Akhenaten was in Atlantis getting the city ready for the pyramid power transfer, you think you stopped."

"I guess I didn't."

"This year, Akhenaten must complete the rejuvenation process."

"What's going to shit him out?" asked Anand with a smile. "A elephant."

"No… a female camel."

"I have got to see that."

"The Prince wants the king to die and take his place as the ruler of Atlantis."

"What's the Tong used for?"

"It is a key that powers the memory transfer into the new cloned host."

"So, King Tut and King Akhenaten need to be reborn this year."

"Yes the original Tong was destroyed at the Giza Pyramids when it exploded. The males need to go through this process every 13 years. The females were in hibernation until you found the ankh. Now the Prince will have a one man orgy after his rebirth with his mothers and bare children that will be cloned."

Or fucked up physically like him. Thought Anand while smiling.

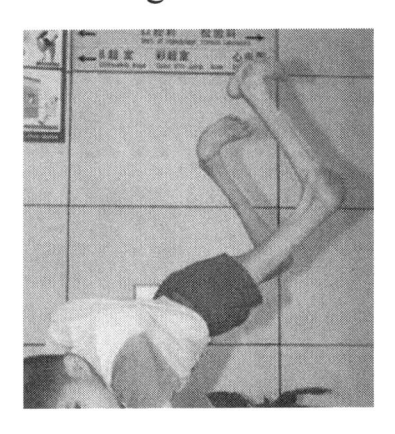

"This is how the population of Atlantis will be reborn."

"From camel asses," sarcastically said Anand. *I can't let that happen.* He thought with concern.

Chapter 9

The **Tong**

The transport began to enter a glass tube as it slightly decended downward. Anand saw five more tubes and became a little frightened but knew help was following his tracking device. He then saw above them a floating ceiling of Arctic ice. His ears began to pop as the transport decended closer and closer to the not-so-lost city of Atlantis.

"How long has Atlantis been here?" asked Anand.

"As long as there has been camels," jokingly said Khaleef. "That is not Atlantis."

"Then where is it?"

"See that long upward vertical tube out your right side window?"

"Yes."

"It leads to Atlantis which is in a ice cave near the surface."

The transport entered the city and stopped in front of a group of men that looked like Saudi Arabian business men wearing Hejazi Turbans and long white Jalabiyas.

"Every government in the world," said Khaleef. "Has agreed to keep the public from entering Antarctica."

"Why?" asked Anand.

"Because they know what we used in retaliation for Admiral Byrd's invasion."

"Operation High Jump."

"Yes, they tried to attack and lost. We knew they were coming back, so we had to send them a message and any other country that wanted to try and invade."

"What was that message?"

"NATO was just formed and had it's first joint naval exercise with many countries involved. We announced prior for them to never return to Antarctica or we would destroy their cities."

"With what?"

"We sent them a sample of our power. King Akhenaten fired a focused beam into the firmament and bounced it back down at the center of that NATO naval exercise, destroying every ship. The Americans covered up the destruction and later announced it was a nuclear bomb test called *Operation Crossroads*. (True) All the families of the dead were paid to keep quiet and the ones that didn't, disappeared of sudden natural causes.

The men all walked through a decontamination chamber and Anand was later pushed into a locked empty room. An hour later a Egyptian women entered with a tray of cooked seafood and a tall blue colored drink.

Anand was starving as he ate the delicious seafood quickly. He then downed the blue drink like a desert lizard, not knowing it was to fertize eggs. Two minutes later his stomach began to ache as he moaned and burped. Canuk entered the locked room holding a white towel. Anand then hunched over in pain and quickly dropped his pants. He then shitted so hard the Tong flew across the room like a missile. Shit flew all over the wall like a fire hose.

Canuk picked up the Tong with the towel and left the room. Anand was laying on the floor with his pants still down to his ankles. He was breathing hard with his eyes closed when he heard multiple sounds coming from the ceiling. He rolled over and saw holes as a spray of sea water showered down on him.

They have done this before. He thought as the sea water began to get warmer.

"You could've asked me to take it out!" yelled Anand as he stood up and pulled his soaked pants up. The water stopped and another Egyptian woman entered with a towel and a red jumpsuit for him to put on.

"Can you help me escape?" he asked her in Arabic. She didn't say a word as she left and the door locked. He put on the jumpsuit and 10 minutes later, the door opened. It was Canuk again and he ordered Anand to follow the Egytian woman as he followed behind him. They entered a large room filled with sand that smelled like elephant shit. To the left of the room was a plastic covered patient's hospital bed and at the right, a large door that was opened as a pregnant camel was escorted on a leash.

"Please don't make me watch this?" he asked Canuk in Arabic. "Earlier I thought I could."

"Close your eyes," he responded. An Egyptian man wearing a white doctors jacket with a stethoscope around his neck, place a glowing glube on the camels swollen stomach.

The camel fell over and began to moan. Then its ass began to swell and Anand closed both of his eyes. Suddenly the camel farted and Anand opened one eye. He was shocked at what he saw next.

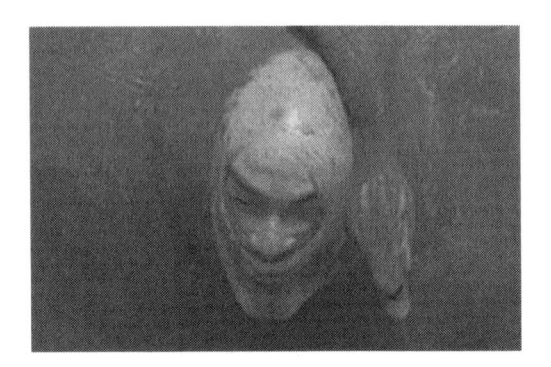

It was a face pushing out the vagina of the camel. Two Egyptian nurses began to help the cloned King Tut, like mid-wives and began to push on the camel's stomach. Tut popped out like a rabbit turd.

He was then placed on the hospital bed and the Egyptian doctor placed a Khepresh helmet over his head. He then placed the Tong in a hole at the top of the crown and the helmet began to glow blue. It pulsated for two minutes and then it was removed. King

Tut opened his eyes and then looked toward Anand.

"Mr. Abbul, this is a day of reclamation. I have reclaimed my extended life thanks to you and now I must decide if you are to be eaten. Tell me a good reason why Canuk should not eat you?"

"Because you promised my wife."

"I promised her…I wouldn't eat you."

"Okay…Sudanese taste nasty," Anand said quickly. "And I returned the Tong. I could have given it to the Canadians."

"We know your negroe Israelite friend was not Canadian, but an American working with the CIA." Anand then frowned. "We also know my father is holding your wife until you return with the Tong."

"Your father Akhenaten told me to say three words in Arabic if you captured me…*Amun Ra Sekhmet*. What does it mean? I said them on the plane in Greenland."

"No!" shouted King Tut as he sat up and pushed away the women that were cleaning him. "Those words reproprammed the Tong and I have only one month before my mind is erased."

"Just fix it," said Anand.

"My father is the only one who knows the code."

"You should ask him nicely for it." Anand was being a asshole and enjoyed it.

"We need you to hide it like you did through airport customs."

"Up my ass?" asked Anand knowing he wasn't going to be eaten. "Only if you turn it off."

"It is already deactivated."

"I'll do it for you."

"Good, my father wants Atlantis back," said Tutenkhaman then waving to a servant. "Get the *Juggernaut* sub ready for tranport. Mr. Abbul you are coming with me to Cairo."

"Thank God," he whispered. Canuk became angry again. Tut grabbed the Tong from the crown and walked naked from the birthing room. He then entered his nearby palace and took a hot shower. Anand just walked in front of Canuk as three naked cloned Egyptian females with see-through red silk robes sat on a circular seating area that surrounded a low flaming fire-pit.

Anand smiled, missing his wife again as his pants began to swell. Tut returned from the shower in his black Jalabiyas while wiping shaving cream from his face with a white towel.

"Mr. Abbul you and your brother are going to assist me in getting that code from my father."

"And how are we going to do that?"

"I need you to kidnap my mother Nefertiti and threaten to kill her at King Piankhi's pyramid."

"Why there?" asked Anand hoping he meant the pretty one.

"I want him to blame Sudan," said Tut knowing his father might bomb them. "If he doesn't return your wife and give you the unlock code. I want you to threaten him with leverage...a wife for a wife. And then kill my mother if he doesn't comply."

Is this motherfucker stupid. Thought Anand. *I am going to get my wife back using leverage and then watch his cripple-ass mind go blank.*

Anand followed as King Tut, Canuk, and four body guards entered a two door elevator. It rose to the surface, to Atlantis that sat in a large ice cave. They all put on winter gear and walked toward the edge of the city that was filled with Egyptian slaves chipping away newly forming ice.

They all then got in a waiting snow tractor and drove through a long tunnel and onto the open frozen desert.

The tractor traveled for an hour and Anand began to see old rusty wreckage of German World War II tanks and planes.

"What happened here?" he asked.
"At the end of World War II, the Germans tried to invade Atlantis," said Tut. "They had already lost the war and wanted to use our transport tubes for an counter attack against the Allies."

"I see they lost that fight too."

"We forced them to retreat back to Argentina."

Twenty minutes later, the snow tractor reached the shore line of the Ronne Ice Shelf.

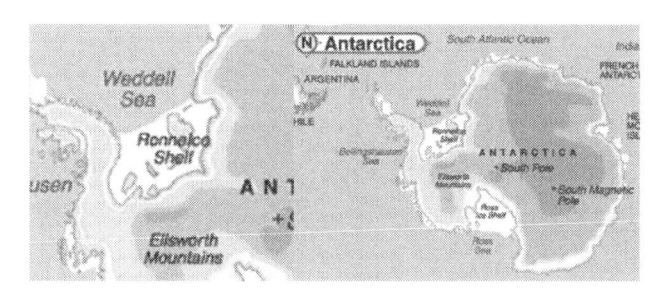

They waited as a submarine *Juggernaut* rose to the surface and broke throught the thin ice layer.

The men got onto the very old but newer looking submarine. Anand was amazed at how quiet it was. They floated slowly and then excellerated at a high speed northward.

The Americans had reestablished a signal with Anand's tracking device and sent a Trident Class sub to follow. It couldn't keep up but manage to project its course and presumed it was heading on a straight path through the Arabian Sea, toward the Gulf of Aden, and then maybe to Egypt.

Chapter 10

The Bet

King Tut entered the sub's mess hall to eat his first real meal with his younger cloned body. He had a worried look on his face as Anand sat with one body guard standing near the entrance hatch, not taking his eyes off of him. Tut sat in front of Anand as a female Egyptian sailor fixed him his usual plate of food.

"Mister Abbul may I join you?"
"Do I have choice to refuse?"
"No."
"Then have a seat."
"I have a story to tell you."
"You people always have a story to tell."
"Quiet and listen."
"Sorry your highness."
"Have you heard of the Anunnaki?"
"I thought you said be quiet…and yes."
"They were believed to have descended from Heaven," said Tut. "And created the first humans."
"They were believed to be winged Gods that helped the Sumerians," said Anand
"Yes, that was us. We flew Atlantis down to Mesopotamia and taught the Sumerians

complexed math and geometrical problem solving."

"I've read about them in college." *You soul-less freak.*

"And do you know that the Sumerians of Mesopotamia, before the Assyrians capture most of the Middle Eastern countries, were all so-called black melatonin skinned people…and they lived in the location of Iraq and Kuwait."

"Yes," said Anand. "And Jesus must've had melatonin skin because he escaped to Egypt from King Herod, to blend in with the local population."

"Arrogant Edomite whites try to change history," said King Tut. "But they are not succeeding in their lies anymore."

"Why did you teach the Sumerians?"

"We needed them to grow in knowledge, to help us build the PTP's. (Power Transfer Pyramids)"

"I'm sorry I had the Americans blow up the Giza Pyramid," said Anand not caring what PTP meant. "But you said you were going to enslave the world."

"I am, but I was ordered by my father sixty years ago to find the missing ankhs."

"In the third dynasty, we sent a Sumerian called Imhotep to Egypt. He built the first pyramid of Djoser. It was not successful in power transferrance."

"You do remember you told me you were a compulsive liar?"

"I just want you too know that we helped the world and in return they helped us."

"The Americans arent helping you."

"They want that weapon we fired on them in 1946. They have been trying for years and now that they are advancing in technology, they are forcing us to make defensive changes. That's why we needed the Giza Pyramid to power up Atlantis."

"What does this history lesson have to do with me?

"Oh…nothing. I have to perform memory exercises every time I'm reborn."

"Okay."

"Do you know the Russians tried to invade Atlantis in 1949? We used our weapon and blew up Chagan Lake in Semipalainski."

"Where's that?"

"In Kazakhstan. We told them to retreat or Moscow was next."

"So the Russians don't have nuclear weapons?" asked Anand.

"They do…just not as powerful as ours."

"So when we get to Egypt…what is the plan?"

"You are to take the Tong to my father and he will reset it to be reborn. Canuk will deliver a message to set up a meeting. You and your brother's men are to steal the Tong back and return it to me."

"And what do I get out of this deal?"

"I will not serve you on a plate and my men will safely rescue your wife."

"Okay…we have a deal," agreed Anand. He was glad to be taken off Canuk's menu. King Tut then snapped his fingers and a guard handed him a small metal box.

"Here is the Tong. We will be at the Port of Ain Sukhna in thirty minutes."

"Where's that?"

"Southeast of Cairo."

"Oh."

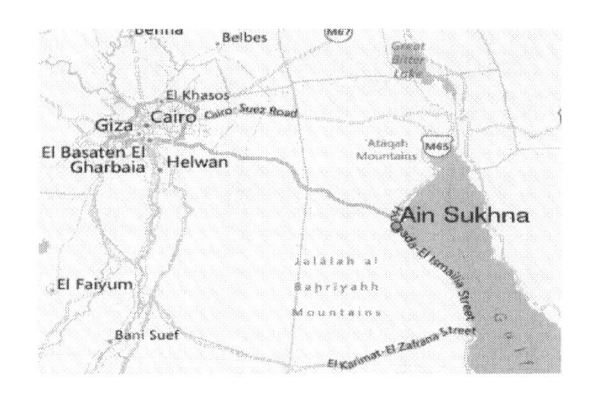

Anand was driven at sundown to King Tut's personal hotel in Cairo. He had a perfect view from his window of the Giza Pyramids. He wished his wife could have been there with him to enjoy the work that was built by Hebrew slaves, that later migrated to West Africa around 300 a.d. (True).

Google-E1B1A

As the sun rose and the morning dew glistened over every plant in Tut's garden, Anand was awakened by Canuk standing over his bed with a knife and fork in each hand.

"Breakfast is ready," said Canuk as Anand jumped from his blanket away from him.

"I thought I was breakfast...the way you are holding that knife scared me."

"I still want....I mean I haven't eaten any humans lately."

"Thank God."

"You have thirty minutes to get dressed and eat, then we are leaving."

"I'll be ready."

Anand was driven to the desert and then rode in the same disguised armored vehicle he rode in to Iran. The wheels retracted into the body of the transport as it floated over the road. Then it veered onto open desert and went supersonic in the direction of Siwa Lake, where the Tahaghien Island sat at the northern part of the oasis.

The transport flew west, close to Al Hawat Highway for four hours and then veered south. Anand became scared and then curious.

"Canuk!" he shouted toward the front passenger seat. "Canuk!"

"Lower your tone."

"Where are we going? This isn't the way to Siwa Lake."

"We are going into battle."

"Battle."

"There has been a change of plans. King Tut has agreed with his father Akhenaten to battle for the Tong."

"Why?" asked Anand, a little scared. "I thought he was going to give it to him."

"King Akhenaten has the Prince's wife hostage and also wants the key to Atlantis."

"I thought he was a nut-less homo?"

"What's a homo?" asked Canuk.

"I should've used the correct term and you should too. He's a faggot...a man that has sex with another man."

"Fugget."

"Yes...faggot."

"The Prince promised his wife he would never sleep with another woman. He has kept his promise."

"Tell do-do dick...fucking men is still cheating."

"What?"

"How did he capture his wife?"

"Her stasis sarcophagus was lost and King Akhenaten found it under the Giza Pyramid. He ordered the Prince to settle their dispute with a battle."

"I didn't agree to fight in his battle."

"If you want your wife...you will fight."

"This is bullshit," whispered Anand. "I need a gun."

"We don't fight with guns to settle our differences."

"Are we having a fist fight?"

"It will be done like the days of old...with swords. The armies of Kush against the Assyrians used swords with honor."

"Stabbing and slicing is not honorable...it

is barbaric. And I don't see any armies." Anand then looked out the front window and saw something in the distance. "I'm not fighting anybody unless I have body armor and a semi-automatic."

The carrier flew up and then roller-coastered down a large sand-dune. Anand became scared as he saw about 100 local Egyptian men standing in row with their backs toward numerous trucks and cars behind them. And on the other side of the flat valley was about the same amount of men. They were all swinging homemade rusty swords and spears as a camel was behind them with King Akhenaten riding it. At that very moment another troop carrier flew in, extended its wheels, and then landed. The Prince exited with a mean look on his face with two body guards. Canuk bowed as the Prince walked up to him.

"Today will be a day to remember."

"Yes my Prince."

"The last sword battle I've witnessed was Shaka Zulu's warriors against the British Army in 1879." (True)

"The British had guns and still lost," said Anand.

"Strategy was their key to victory and it will be mine today."

"I don't see a strategy," said Anand. "I

only see two rows of angry men."

"The weak will sacrifice themselves first as my strongest fighters will step back. Canuk begin the attack."

"I'm strong too," said Anand "I'll just hang back here."

The first wave of about fifty men began to run toward King Akhenaten's little army. He then signaled his men to attack. All one hundred and seven of his men began to run and scream, "ALLAHU AKBAR!" The first wave of Tutankhamun's men were sliced apart like ripe tomatoes. Blood and body parts were everywhere as Anand hunched over and through-up breakfast. Akhenaten's men then continued running toward the rest of Tut's men.

"Now you will see my father's defeat in one swift stroke."

Anand looked up and the carnage began again. The Prince's strategy didn't work. His whole little army was killed in fifteen minutes.

He had forgotten the one advantage that

Akhenaten used, it was *Crack Cocaine*. His men were all given the addictive drug all week long. And it made them lethargically fearless, not to mention they were motivated with the promise that they would receive a double hit after the battle. The drug induced men with dilated pupils screamed in victory while drunkenly waving their swords in the air.

The Prince drove a dead slaves pickup truck to Akhenaten and gave him the Tong that was in the same metal box. He then bowed to his father and handed him what looked like a gold scepter with an ankh on the end. In actuality…it was the key that powered Atlantis. Anand knew he saw it before. He just couldn't remember where.

The King then said something to Tut as Anand read his lips at a distance while standing next to Canuk. *Your wife is safe in Atlanta.*

"In Atlanta Georgia?" whispered Anand with a confused look on his face. "Is the Prince going to America?"

"No, King Akhenaten and his wives lived at Atlanta under Siwa Lake."

"Oh…now I remember."

"And the Tong is the key to him having children."

"Yes, from a camel's ass," Anand said sarcastically.

"And yours," said Canuk.

"What?"

"Oh nothing."

Anand then remembered where he saw the scepter Tut gave his father. It was on a tablet at the museum in Germany.

Ankh **Tong** Scepter

Chapter 11

Revenge and Rescue

The Prince drove back through the battle area with his tires soaked with blood and sand that sprayed across both sides of the truck.

"Get in," yelled King Tut. "We are going to get my wife."

Don't you mean your sister? Thought Anand while smiling. Tut drove frantically as the flying armored transport moved toward Akhenaten, to fly him to Atlantis.

Three hour later, they reached the center of the resort, to the water reservoir and the elevator rose, anticipating their arrival. Tut's bride exited in a beautiful white dress.

He ran to her while limping and gave her a big hug and kiss. Then he yelled to Canuk.

"Bring him here!"

"Yes my Prince." Canuk then grabbed Anand and began dragging him toward the elevator.

"What's going on?" shouted Anand as he resisted.

"Be grateful Mr. Abbul," said Tut. "You are the father of our new race."

"What race...father...what?" he shouted a little confused. "I haven't slept with no one but my wife." *After I was married.*

"You are carrying my growing embryos in your rectum that must be implanted into hundreds of camels."

"And what happens if they're not?" asked Anand.

"They grow quickly into beings that are blood thirsty."

I am going to have the widest asshole in the world. Thought Anand realizing Tut didn't get the Tong code.

"My father accepted my revenge plan from the beginning...for you almost killing me at the Giza Pyramid."

"So, needing the code was a lie?"

"I did say I was a liar." Anand became angry. "You were slowly inseminated by the

Tong, and that is the beginning process that has been done for thousands of years. But instead of one clone, you will be harvesting hundreds of them."

"Are you telling me…I'm a tadpole?"

"A what?"

"Oh nothing," said Anand.

"Goodbye Mr. Abbul, and my father is keeping his promise. Your wife is safe in Atlanta and waiting for you after the birthing."

Anand stopped resisting Canuk and walked toward the glass elevator. It went down as he began to throw up, knowing he was being used like a flatworm parasite (Ribeiroia). He rode the elevator down lost in thought.

I'm going to be a human bird that shits clones out my ass and probably have to watch my kids get pushed out of a female camel's hairy smelly pussy.

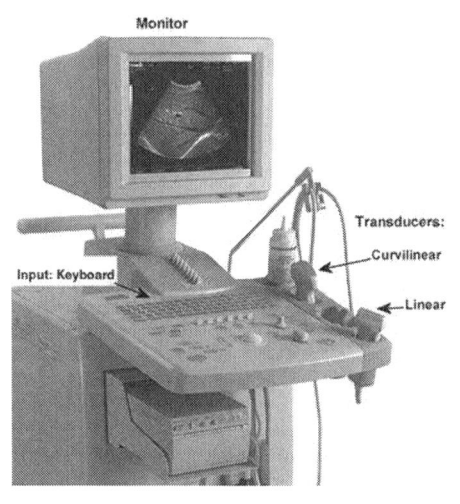

The door opened and Anand was escorted to a medical examination room. *I'm going to be a dad.* He thought while undressing to get an ultrasound. He had to lay on his stomach as an Egyptian nurse ran the Transducer Probe down his spine. It picked up numerous tiny fertilized humanoid embryos and something else big in his anal cavity. Anand looked over at the monitor.

"Is that why my ass itches like a crack addict?"

The nurse explained the process that was going to happen to him and it calmed his nerves down. She assured Anand that he wouldn't feel a thing and the itching would stop.

Nafy walked in two minutes later and Anand was still on his stomach with his ass cheeks exposed. She became upset.

"What happened...did you get raped?"

"No...I have an infection. I mean infestation."

"What?"

"They have chosen me to be their surrogate mother."

"Are you having a baby out of your bum-bum?"

"No," smile Anand. "I just have to go to the restroom and take a liquid dump." His stomach began pulsating. "Nurse!" he yelled while looking at his lumpy vibrating belly. "I need a bed with stirrups!"

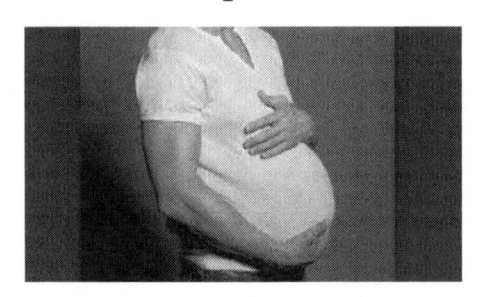

"I'll wait in the lobby," said scared Nafy, not wanting any part of what was going to happen next.

"Yes dear," said Anand while running to the restroom. Before Nafy could exit the room, Anand screamed like a little girl. Then Nafy heard a liquid splash down that indicated he was not on a toilet, but over a bucket.

"My ass is burning!" he yelled as Nafy smiled. "You Egyptians are all liars, like your prince." Then something heavy fell out of his ass. "What the fuck is that?" he shouted.

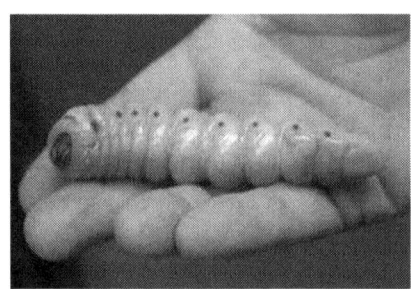

The Egyptian nurse picked up the bucket while reaching in it. "It's the placenta casing that carried the embryos."

"Are you going to give me a super postpartum huge maxi-pad for my bleeding ass vagina?"

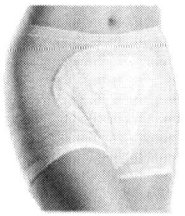

"What?"

"I was being sarcastic," Anand said in Arabic.

"*Ayreh Feek*" whispered the nurse.

"Fuck you too" he responded in English.

The nurse left the room with the placenta and Anand quickly had to shit again. He hunched over in pain again and then shitted a burning pile of Tut's embryos into the bucket.

Anand decided to put his clothes back on. *I'm getting the fuck out of here.* He thought while pulling up his pants. He then took the bucket and poured the embryos down the toilet and flushed.

Anand ran out of the room, down the hall, and grabbed Nafy's arm. "We are getting out of here," he said with concern while looking for the hall that led to the elevator. All of a sudden an alarm began to sound.

Anand became scared again and they ran as fast as they could through the underwater city as two guards chased them. They reached the same elevator to the surface and managed to get the door closed before the guards reached them. Oh shit…I feel like I'm going to explode again," said Anand as Nafy backed up. He hunched over then pulled his pants down as Nafy saw his ass-hole dilate to the size of a car exhaust pipe. He then sprayed the whole elevator wall with green colored shit. Nafy almost threw up while holding her nose closed.

The elevator door opened twenty seconds later and the sunlight blinded both of them. They covered their eyes while running toward a bus with tourist getting off at the front of the resort.

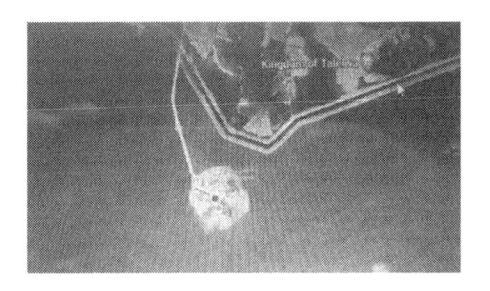

"What was going on down there?" asked Nafy.

"Some freaky shit. Let's run for that *Black and White* taxi and ask the driver can we borrow his cell phone.

Twenty minutes later, the taxi was heading north on Siwa Road.

Then out of nowhere, a white unmarked helicopter landed on the highway, blocking the taxi. Tyrone jumped out and Anand was relieved.

"It is damn good to see you," shouted Anand.

"Who is this?" asked Nafy.

"It's my old college roommate from America."

"Hello Mrs. Abbul…and you are a hard man to track." Anand gave him a man hug. Then they both got onto the white helicopter as Tyrone paid the taxi driver. He then ran and got in the front seat of the helicopter while putting on a communication headset.

"Anand, you are one lucky Sudanese. They were going to feed you to those things that came out of your ass."

"Like a spider?" asked Anand. "And how did you know that?"

"That tracking device we put in you also transmits sound."

"Did you hear my ass spray green shit all over that elevator?"

"I didn't but Langley probably did."

The helicopter flew for one hour to a secret American base disguised as an oil refinery in the middle of the Egyptian desert.

Tyrone, Nafy, and Anand all flew on a C-17 and flown to refuel stops at Avianno Air Base in Spain, Loring Air Force Base in Maine, and then to Scott Air Force Base in Illinois.

It was the shortest route on the flat earth map to reach America in straight lines.

Tyrone was ordered to escort and protect Anand until the city under the resort was under American control or destroyed. He knew the one place that they would be safe.

The three of them flew on a chartered flight to Chicago, where his mother Grace lived.

They reached the house on a Saturday afternoon and they all got out of an unmarked FBI black Chevy Suburban as Tyrone turned to Anand.

"Remember what I told you about my mom and I also forgot to tell you…she has a little dementia?"

"Yeah I do too."

"And don't mention the Koran or anything religious." Tyrone then turned to Nafy. "You will get a lecture on hair care…just ignore her."

They all walked up the steps to a small bricked ranch style house with flowers planted all along the front. Tyrone rang the doorbell and a young dark skinned female opened the door.

"Hi," Tyrone said while pausing,

wondering who the woman was. "Who are you?"

"I'm Mrs. Johnson's housekeeper," she said opening the door wider.

"Is that my baby!" yelled his mother from the den. They all entered the house as the smell of collard greens filled the air. "Come give your momma some sugar."

"It's good to see you Ma. These are my friends that I told you about. This is Anand and his wife Nafy." They stood in the entry way of the den while sniffing the unknown food fragrance. "This is my mother Grace."

"Come in, let me get a good look at-cha," she said while waving. "You two don't look like the Arabs on television. Tyrone, I thought you said they were Arabs?"

"Forgive my mother. No Ma…I said they were from Sudan."

"We are Muslim," said Anand as Tyrone stared at him angrily.

"This country will unwillingly indoctrinate you two into Christianity and there's nothing wrong with that. But I believe it is a form of control. Go to an all-white church and stay the whole service…then go to one of ours. They have taken everything away from us, but there is one thing they can't. Do you know what that is young lady?"

"No ma'am I don't."

"They can't take away the *Holy Spirit* that is in us."

"Ma, how's your sore feet?" Tyrone asked to change the subject.

"They're better. Do you know black Jesus washed the feet of his disciples?" (John 13: 5) "And this new housekeeper won't even cut my toe nails."

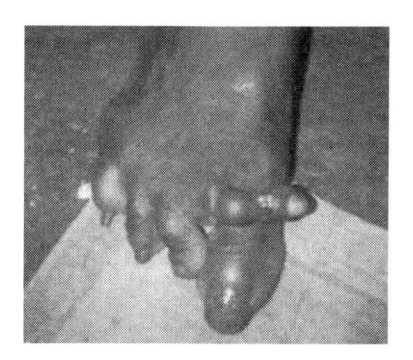

"Ma, she is paid to clean the house."

"Anando, did you know we built the White House?"

"Ma, we didn't build the White House."

"I'm not talking about that *Ivanwald Dorm* full of young brainwashed boys that clean the *Cedar White House* for that secret evangelist Doug Coe. (Was True) His devout obsession with white Jesus (Cesare Borgia) was so deep that he had special printed *Jesus* bibles with only the books of *Mathew, Mark, Luke, John*, and the last one called *Acts of Ambassadors*. (True) If he had read Deuteronomy 28:68…it would've changed his one-sided views."

"Ma...please, not the story about the Christian Mafia again."

"Yes...and there's soon to be a peach colored white man in the White House. What was I talking about?"

"Oh yeah, the Israelites built the Giza Pyramids and the White House."

"Ma, we are going shopping...we should be back in a couple of hours."

"Miss Nappy, do you know who you are?"

"It's Nafy and yes, I am Sudanese."

"How about you, Anando?"

"I am the same."

"You two are also lost like my little Tyrone. I want you both to *Google* **E1B1A** and when you understand what this is...explain it to my Tyrone. And tell him the *Christian Mafia* runs this country, not the Illuminuties...I mean the Illuminati."

"Yes Ma'am," said Anand believing it was *crazy* not dementia she was suffering from.

Chapter 12

The Ride to A-Town

Tyrone drove Nafy and Anand to the only mall he knew before he went to college, to find some clothes for them to wear.

"What the hell has happened to this place?" Tyrone asked himself." I use to go here all the time."

"It looks like Damascus, Syria," said Nafy. "Before the bombings."

Syria

"I know a good clothing store downtown

for men and women."

"What store?" asked Anand.

"It's called Express."

"Do they make you buy clothes fast?" asked Nafy.

"No, and they are not expensive."

"My husband has plenty of money."

"We can't use his credit card. It is traceable...I'll pay for your clothes."

Tyrone drove toward the highway in order to get to downtown Chicago. Anand sat in the back seat behind Nafy. He then leaned forward looking at Tyrone.

"Remember that day we were looking out the dorm window and those five dumb ass white boys were trying to sail a paper boat in a puddle?"

"Yeah...it took three seconds for it to sink," said Tyrone. "Then they tried to fight that black dude walking back to his dorm."

"He kicked all five of their asses," said Anand.

"I guess that Angel dust didn't work?"

"Tut told me Atlantis was sinking when a engine boiler exploded on the 15th of April, 1912. (Same date Titanic sank.) An Egyptian cook snapped and began raping the women in the kitchen stock room. The women that were not raped called him the (S.S.R.) *Sinking-Ship-Rapist*."

"That is sick."

"Atlantis didn't sink and he was punished," said Anand. "He had a choice of being castrated or walk the plank."

"Did he lose his nuts?"

"No...that dumb ass said he couldn't live without his testicles so he took his chances walking the plank."

"What happen?"

"A giant squid wrapped his tentacles around him and bit his head off."

"I would've lost my nuts and brought a pump."

"What pump?" asked Nafy.

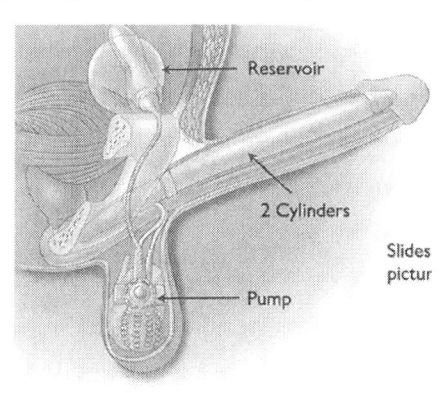

Tyrone drove onto the last highway into the city and his cell phone began ringing.

"Hello." Anand stared out the side window as Nafy listened on. "Yes sir...what...oh no...yes sir...right away." He hung up with a concern look on his face. Anand leaned forward.

"Was that call about us?"

"Yes, your King Tut just bombed the Fukushima Nuclear Power Plant in Japan," Tyrone said while glancing back.

"He has threatened to bomb the SM-1 Nuclear Power Plant in Washington D.C. when they come in range."

"Why?" asked Nafy.

"They want Anand and me."

"They are going to eat you," said Nafy.

"No, I flushed their kids down the toilet and they probably want me to breed them some more," said Anand. "And I took a shit in their elevator…twice."

"They are definitely going to eat you," simultaneously said Tyrone and Nafy.

"We are ordered to catch a flight out of O'Hara," said Tyrone. "Nafy you will be flown back to Sudan."

"I'm not leaving my husband anymore. I'm going…where he's going."

"It is not up to me. I just follow orders."

"You better get on that phone and call someone in charge or we aren't flying anywhere."

Tyrone made a phone call and confirmed that Nafy was allowed to go with Anand. He drove them to O'Hara Air Reserve Station and they were put onboard a KC-135 Air Refueling Aircraft.

After refueling a squadron of F-16's that were flying across country, the KC-135 diverted to *Bed-3-Area*, Egypt. It was a fake oil company in the middle of the desert that hid a fully staffed U.S. military base.

They landed twenty two hours later and

were fed at the base cafeteria. Anand was ordered to go alone to speak to the Commander of Base Operations.

Tyrone walked up to sad Nafy with his tray of food and sat across from her.

"Anand has been through a lot," he said calmly. "And I'm not going to say with confidence…that we are getting out of this alive. I don't know why they want me or what's going to happen."

"I need you to watch and protect Anand as best as you can."

"I will…he's my friend."

"What are they asking him?"

"He is being debriefed and then given instructions as to when and where an extraction might take place."

"Shouldn't you be there?"

"I have a different task, but I'll see that he is heading back home before I complete my mission."

"I assume you guys are going back to Siwa Lake?"

"No…we are going to Atlantis. That's all I can tell you."

"I'm not staying here."

"You are being flown home," said Tyrone while digging in his pocket. "Here...this is a GT-800 worldwide mini-cell phone and I need you to wait for my call. I'll let you know when Anand is safe."

"You better."

Blackhawk Helicopter

And why are most American Army helicopters named after Indians? It was because of an Army Regulation 70-28 which has been rescinded.

Anand and Tyrone were put on a Blackhawk helicopter and flown to the opposite side of Siwa Lake near an awaiting hovering heavily armored personnel carrier that just extended its wheels. It was different, more armed and Tyrone was sure they were going to shoot the helicopter right out of the sky.

The two men slowly walked toward the armor vehicle as the Blackhawk lifted off leaving a cloud of sand behind them. The back door slowly opened and Canuk walked out. He was licking his lips and Anand knew they were going to eat Tyrone. He knew all black men in movies got killed first. *It's the same for this book he thought.* ☺ The men were pushed onto the carrier and buckled in. The vehicle then rolled fifty feet before retracting its wheels and flying toward the a different docked sub destined for Atlantis.

Anand was seated next to Tyrone and leaned his head towards him.

"I don't think you are going to make it out of this situation alive."

Deep Blue / Samuel Jackson gets eaten by a shark at the beginning of the movie.

"Why are you saying that?"

"American movies."

"Oh...well this isn't a movie and I plan on fighting for my life."

"I'm not giving you inevitable bad news," said Anand.

"Buddy, do you know why black Americans don't go to the doctor?"

"No health insurance."

"That is one reason," said Tyrone. "They don't want to hear bad news that they are dying or will be dead at a specific time."

"We all don't want bad news."

"Yeah, but black people have learned to live life to the fullest under harsh conditions for hundreds of years. In the 1970's there was a mass incarceration of black men into the prison system. That left single mom's at home raising kids, many on Welfare."

"What's Welfare?"

"Government assistance to feed and house the poor."

"I read about that."

"Well, many kids grew up poor and learned to survive by enjoying life one day at a time." Tyrone paused as a loud noise was heard. It was a sonic boom as the transport increased its speed. "Many blacks decide that it is better to enjoy life up until they die, not go to the hospital and hear bad news that they have six months to a year to live."

"So what you are saying is that your people live day to day partying instead of trying to fight death if given a time limit."

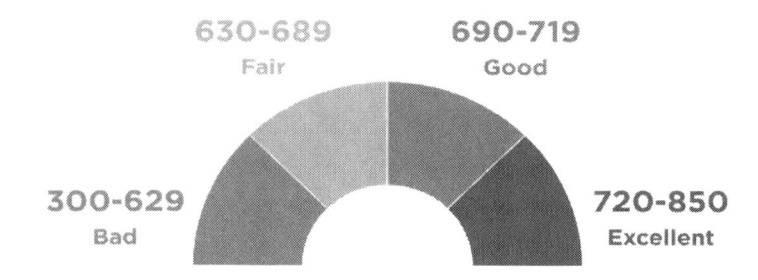

630-689
Fair

690-719
Good

300-629
Bad

720-850
Excellent

"Yes...we also don't give a shit about **credit** or a **score**...unless we are trying to buy a house."

"Your mother asked us...who we are?"

"She sometimes doesn't know who she is," said Tyrone.

"You must listen to her if we survive, I mean *you* survive. God has given her a gift."

"Dementia is not a gift...it's a curse upon an aging body."

"I just thought of how we can defeat these Atlantians before they breed a new race in my ass."

"How?"

"My King Piankhi defeated the Egyptians because they had no leadership. They only had divided groups of warlords throughout Egypt."

"How does that have anything to do with us?"

"Egypt is in the middle of a revolution against Hosni Mubarak."

"And?"

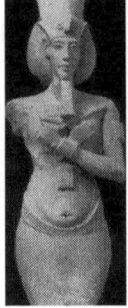

"We just have to get the Egyptian people to turn against Tut and his sissy looking dad. He already has the government on his side. We just have to get the public to revolt on him."

"How do we do that?"

"My German girlfriend told me President Mubarak had 17 million dollars of stolen government funds in a German Bank account, and he tried to buy the bust of Queen Nefertiti for King Tut. That money was for the Egyptian Children's Cancer Foundation."

"We just have to get this information to the Egyptian public," said Tyrone. "That Tut is trying to purchase the head of his mother with tax funds that were stolen for cancer stricken Egyptian children."

"We have to advertise," said Anand.

"The CIA is good at spreading disinformation. I'll make a few phone calls if we survive."

Leaflets being released from Blackhawk.

Chapter 13

Run

The armored carrier slowed its speed for twenty minutes before reaching the submarine that waited for their arrival. Anand and Tyrone were locked together in the subs brig (Jail).

"Hey dude, where is that G800 cell phone?" asked Anand.

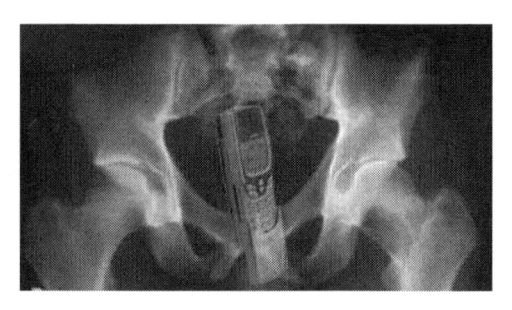

"It's where you hid that weed when that cop ordered you out of that marijuana smoke filled rest room."

"That phone's going to give you colon cancer."

"At least it's smaller than that Tong."

"When did you see the Tong?"

"We have special intercept computers that hack the radiation thermal scanners in Cairo. I was sent a composite picture to my cell phone."

"Are you saying that thing is radioactive?"

"Just a harmful low dose."
"It did vibrate in my ass."
"And you liked it…you closet homo."
"Fuck you Tyrone."

The next day when the sub arrived at Atlantis's underwater docking bay, Anand was taken separately to a special birthing room. He was scared they were going to shove the radioactive **Tong** back up his ass and impregnate him again. He was handcuffed to a hospital bed and a female Egyptian nurse entered the room.

"Are you going to rape me for my sperm?" he asked in Arabic.

"No."

"If you want to extract some manually, I will allow a hand job." The nurse frowned as she uncapped a long needle. "You better not stick that thing in my nuts."

"I am only withdrawing blood."

"Oh thank Allah."

"From your liver." Two strong male interns came in and held Anand still. The nurse felt down his ribcage to the bottom bone and then aimed the needle on his left side while angling upward.

"Shouldn't you have an ultra-sound to guide that?" asked Anand. "How about sterile gauze soaked in alcohol to clean my skin?"

"Hold him still." She then slowly began to insert the needle and Anand screamed at the top of his lungs.

"Mr. Abbul…I haven't broken the skin yet."

"Oh, I thought you were in deep." She then pushed the long needle in and he only felt a pinch. It was when he saw the tube fill with blood that made him pass out.

"Sissy ass Sudanese," said the nurse as the interns laughed.

Anand woke up five minutes later on the bed in the brig. He had fallen asleep after he fainted and woke up with a pain in his chest. *I wonder what they are doing to Tyrone?* He asked himself while sitting up on the edge of the bed. King Tut was using Anand's blood with the only embryo found that he didn't flush down the toilet and combine it with Tyrone's sperm to create a super human Atlantian. Tut named the unborn child *Black Camel*. Which was kind of true since he was going to be born from a camel's ass.

Tyrone was dragged back to the brig by both arms. He was thrown in while holding his nuts with both hands. "Are you alright buddy?"

"I'll be okay...they took sperm from my nuts the hard way."

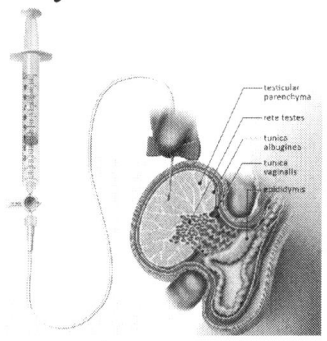

"Let me guess...they used a long needle."

"And a hard handed doctor that had a tight man-grip," Tyrone said while squirming. "If I see him again, I'm kicking him right between his legs."

"I thought of a plan to escape," said Anand. "We just have to get to the transport tubes that travel to the center of the Earth."

"You are talking about the North Pole."

"Yes...I'll scream and ask to be taken to see Akhenaten. You will act like your sleeping and when he opens the door, I'll hold him long enough for you to knock him out."

"How about I hold him and you knock him out."

"What?" said Anand "Why can't you do it?"

"I am not being put on their menu if we're caught again."

"I thought you were a fearless CIA agent."

"Okay, I'll punch him, but do you remember what my *Major* was in college."

"Oh shit...it was Theater Arts 103."

"I was an *Affirmative Action* intern then hired on at the Pentagon as a *Liaison to the Secretary General of the Airforce*. I just electronically pushed documents to various offices."

Pentagon   CIA-HQ Langley Virginia

"Are you telling me...you were just a secretary?"

"Kind of."

"Then how did you get the Air Force to bomb the Giza Pyramid so fast?"

"They were following Tut by satellite and when the pyramid began glowing, they already had birds in the air."

"Birds?"

"Armed fighter jets."

"I was sent to Greenland because of my acting skills."

I thought I was a sissy. Thought Anand. *He's worse than me.* "When I jump him, you run up, punch him in the stomach, and then I'll push him to the floor."

"Okay...but do you *really know* where the transport tubes are?"

"We just have to go down two levels."

"Okay...I'll get in position on the bed."

"Guard...guard!" Anand yelled in Arabic.

The guard slowly walked toward the locked jail.

"I need to see King Akhenaten. This sleeping black ass fucking American has told me...I have a tracking device implanted in me and the U.S. Navy is going to attack." Tyrone angrily glanced up at Anand, hearing only black ass American. The guard opened the cell door and Anand jumped straight at him. Tyrone slowly got up as the guard began to kick Anand's ass like a pedophile's first day in prison. Tyrone slowly walked up to the guard and knocked him out with one punch.

"What took you so long?"

"My black ass American nuts still hurt."

"I thought you weren't so tough?"

"Did I fool ya…I mean was my acting believable?"

"It was and I called you a bitch ass nigga."

"Hey…slow your roll," said Tyrone. "We're not in college anymore. But if you were white, you know that's an automatic ass whooping. Ask those white people that used that word angrily toward any black person. They didn't get very far and in good health."

"Let's get out of here…Mr. sensitive," said Anand. They began to **run** and sneak around corners. They made it to a lower flight of stairs and Anand remembered where the tubes were. He ran first and entered the chamber as one transport just arrived. Four Egyptians in military officer uniforms were being escorted to a meeting. Anand and Tyrone jumped in unnoticed and hit the return switches and buckled in.

"We made it," said Tyrone.

"Hey buddy," said Anand after thinking about the n-word. "I read that Boston is the most prejudice state in America."

Boston, Mass.

April 1976 / Ted Landsmark was stabbed with the American Flag.

"I think it is."

"Then why do the people in the south only eat white eggs? Shouldn't the racist white Bostonians eat white eggs and not brown eggs?"

"It's the taste and what chickens are used. Not the color of the eggs. Then again…they are very prejudice. I bet you they call brown eggs…nigger eggs. I do know one thing," said Tyrone. "Their white women love eating some brown skin." He smiled for a second until. "Did you feel that?"

"What?" asked Anand. The tube then began to shake. "Is it an earthquake?"

"I don't know."

"Can you pull that phone out your butt and

see if you can get a signal?"
"I'll be right back."

What they didn't know was Atlantis was flying away. It had the energy thanks to Tutankhamun starting the Giza pyramid that transferred enough power to levitate the city.

Two hours had past when the transport stopped at a port call East Point Plantation. It was a small British island in the middle of the Indian Ocean. Tyrone was not thrilled hearing plantation. He was just glad to not see cotton or sugar-cane fields.

They both got out of the transport and walked topside to see where they were. They realized it was an abandoned island and returned to the transport.

"Have you heard of East Point Plantation?"

"No...but I've visited East Point, Georgia. It's a small town south of Atlanta."

The men continued their journey northward as Tyrone continued to check for a signal. Four hours had past and the transport stopped at an unknown location. They reached the surface at a secret exit and realized they were in India. Tyrone got a signal and called Washington. They informed him that they did not have control of the city under Siwa Lake and Atlantis had rose, flew, and, disappeared from its ice cave under the cover of night. They also informed him of his location.

"Anand, we are in New Delhi."

"New Delhi...isn't it in the middle of India?"

"North India, close to Pakistan," said Tyrone.

"Nafy always wanted to see the Taj Mahal...can you call her?"

"I'll try." Tyrone dialed the other cell

phone number he gave her and there was no answer. "She isn't picking up."

"Let's get back to the transport," Anand said a little worried. "I hope she is okay?"

"The two of them restarted the transport and felt the vibration again.

"Anand, we have tunnels like this everywhere under the United States."

"Why?"

"I guess the military learned a valuable lesson after getting their ass kicked by the Vietcong in the 70's."

"What did they learn?"

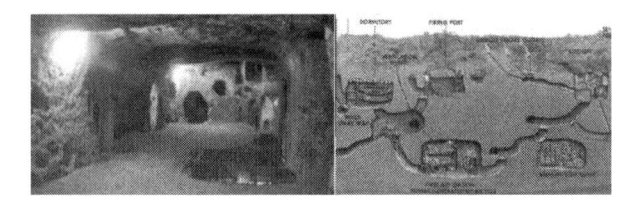

"North Vietnamese dug underground cities for years under Hanoi and in most areas of Vietnam. We bombed the crap out of them and they still kept attacking from underground mazes." Tyrone then paused. "If the U.S. is invaded…we can mobilize from anywhere. That's why the public and enemy satellites in low earth orbit never see large movements of troops and equipment across American highways. Only newly built tanks that get to ride on trains."

They were thirty minutes into the ride when the lights flickered and then went out. Red emergency lights came on and then the transport began to slowly stop. There was an eerie silence as a slight vibration was felt again. Tyrone unbuckled from his seat and placed his ear on the window.

"Anand, strap in tighter."

"What did you hear?" asked Anand.

"It sounded like waves of water. We are about to get pushed."

Suddenly water filled the tube and violently pushed the transport forward. Instead of being moved by the Earth's magnetic poles, they were being pushed by ocean water. The transport became a bullet in an air rifle.

"Tyrone, when we reach the end of this tube, we are going to hit that wall of ice in Greenland."

"I'll try to call Langley and have the military blow a hole in the tube close to any ships in the area."

"That sounds like a plan and thanks for being a good friend, if we don't make it."

Tyrone began dialing his secure number as Anand quietly recited prayers from the Quran, and then a special one for Tyrone.

(2 Sura 122)

"Langley is going to help us," said Tyrone. "They said to stay in the transport."

"You know," said Anand. "Your people are the same ones that failed to overthrow Gaddafi's government."

"There's one thing the CIA doesn't do, and that is…give up on its people. They'll find a way to save us."

The transport began to slow its speed and the men knew something had happened. Then the water stopped pushing the transport. They were baffled and just stared at each other, wondering what was going to happen next.

Ten hours had past and the air was getting thin as the men knew death was closing in on them.

"I guess we're going to die down here," stated Anand. "It's getting harder to breathe."

"Don't give up yet," said Tyrone. "You are a famous man in your country and the U.S. government wants you alive."

"Why, because I'm the mother of a new

race. My ass pussy is still hurting." Tyrone laughed.

"You know…all of this you've seen and heard is top secret. You are bound under the *Non-Verbal International Non-Disclosure Act* prohibiting you to speak about anything pertaining to Antarctica."

"We'll be dead in an hour so that doesn't matter," said Anand while gasping. "I have kept my mouth shut for the past two years."

"We know…you've been on our surveillance watch-list for some time now."

Then in front of the transport a dim light seemed to get brighter in the distance.

"I hope that's not Tut's Egyptian slaves coming to rescue us," said Anand.

"I hope not…or you're going to have more babies."

"It's the US Navy," shouted Anand while coughing."

Tyrone stood up as Anand unbuckled from his seat.

Two Navy Seals in diving suits reached the front window of the transport. They opened a front emergency hatch and handed the men each, a one size-fits-all diving suit and *Hydreliox* air bottles that were a mixture of hydrogen, helium, and oxygen for deep sea diving.

"You men have four minutes to get this gear on because this side of the tube is going to be flooded with sea water."

"Where are we going?"

"Sir, get the gear on quickly," said the lead diver.

The men got the gear on and waited in the transport as the water began to flow and fill the tube in the front of the transport. They all checked each other's pressure regulators an Anand became dizzy again. Then they all waited as the lead diver opened the front hatch. There was a thud and then the water flooded into the transport quickly. The men exited the hatch and began to walk down the water filled tube. They reached an opening in the tunnel and spotted what was once a special plastic cover that dissolved over a hole in the wall and allowed the sea water to enter. (How did the divers get in?) Fifty feet from the opening was a waiting Trident class nuclear submarine.

Anand smiled knowing he was going home. Then he remembered the whole ordeal beginning with him digging into King Piankhi's mummy and retrieving the ass dildo, he meant Tong. Later, the men were informed they were trapped below the Norwegian Sea close to Iceland.

Tyrone called Nafy after he was debriefed and three hours later, the sub stopped close to the coastline near Thule Air Base in Greenland. There, both men rode a rubber raiding craft onto shore.

Later, they were flown on a private military aircraft to the Pentagon in Washington D.C to be debriefed.

Epilogue

A week later, Anand left Washington and arrived back home to his wife in Khartoum under the protection of the United States government. He decided he was never leaving his country ever again.

Atlantis had risen from its snow cave causing ice to fall on all six transport tunnels that flooded throughout the world. Anand and Tyrone were lucky because a section of their tunnel in Antarctica collapsed and closed off rushing in sea water.

Atlantis flew away from Antarctica and was nowhere to be found as the small city under Siwa Lake was destroyed under the cover of night by a U.S. top secret sub launched land to sea missile. It skimmed the surface terrain of the desert and hit its target underwater 100 miles away (161 kilometers) from the Mediterranean Sea.

The *City of Atlantis* hid under a remote area of West Africa and Akhenaten and his cripple son Tutankhamen wanted to build an army of super humans with Tyrone's sperm but needed Anand's children he flushed down a toilet to complete the process.

Two weeks later, around fifty creatures crawled from Siwa Lake on the opposite side of the resort. Their eyes glowed in the night as they began to lethargically walk into the open desert, towards Algeria.

The creatures slowly walked while sniffing constantly for warm blooded animals. Their first night they feasted on mostly Jerboa mice, one Fennec fox, and the dead carcass of a cheetah eaten fly infested gazelle. They had an internal drive to breed and reach Atlantis first, then eat all the people for not finishing their reclamation process into normal Atlantians. Anger filled their half souls for not growing them in the womb of an Egyptian desert camel, but instead a sewer pipe that emptied shit and piss into Lake Siwa.

The End.

"Time is the enemy in obtaining all truths."

Michael K. Jones

Michael's other Books

Profiling or Prejudice and Mumbai Spy are dirty but funny.

King Piye is clean version, **King Piankhi** is not. **(Same story)**

Made in the USA
Columbia, SC
11 October 2022